A nurse by vocation—that's Dido Alexander, Staff Nurse in charge of Men's Medical at St Benedict's and loved by one and all. All, that is, except for dashing new consultant Dr James Dauntcey, who doesn't seem to value her as a nurse—or a woman!

*Books you will enjoy
in our Doctor Nurse series:*

NURSE ON THE SCENE by Lindsay Hicks
ISLAND DOCTOR by Clare Lavenham
TABITHA IN MOONLIGHT by Betty Neels
MARINA'S SISTER by Barbara Perkins
EXAMINE MY HEART, DOCTOR by Lisa Cooper
INTENSIVE AFFAIR by Ann Jennings
NURSE IN DOUBT by Denise Robertson
ITALIAN NURSE by Lydia Balmain
PRODIGAL DOCTOR by Lynne Collins
THE HEALING PROCESS by Grace Read
DREAMS ARE FOR TOMORROW by Frances Crowne
LIFE LINES by Meg Wisgate
DOCTOR MATTHEW by Hazel Fisher
NURSE FROM THE GLENS by Elisabeth Scott
SISTER STEPHANIE'S WARD by Helen Upshall
SISTER IN HONG KONG by Margaret Barker
THE PROFESSOR'S DAUGHTER by Leonie Craig
THE CAUTIOUS HEART by Judith Worthy
NURSE HELENA'S ROMANCE by Rhona Trezise
A SURGEON'S LIFE by Elizabeth Harrison
RING FOR A NURSE by Lisa Cooper
DOCTOR IN THE ANDES by Dana James
DR ARROGANT, MD by Lindsay Hicks

BELOVED ANGEL

BY

LUCINDA OAKLEY

MILLS & BOON LIMITED
15–16 BROOK'S MEWS
LONDON W1A 1DR

*First published in Great Britain 1984
by Mills & Boon Limited*

© Lucinda Oakley 1984

*Australian copyright 1984
Philippine copyright 1984
This edition 1984*

ISBN 0 263 74864 2

Set in 10 on 11½ pt Linotron Times
03–1184–53,500

*Photoset by Rowland Phototypesetting Ltd
Bury St Edmunds, Suffolk
Made and printed in Great Britain by
Richard Clay (The Chaucer Press) Ltd
Bungay, Suffolk*

CHAPTER ONE

DIDO Alexander walked from the warmth of the hospital into the chill air outside. She was tired and hungry and could not wait to get back to the flat she shared with another staff nurse, Millie Simpson, just a short walk away. She had come on duty in the dark and was leaving in the dark; St Benedict's, monumental, all lights ablaze, was like an ocean-going liner behind her. Still, after tomorrow, it was going to be 'nights' for a week, which would be a change.

Dido pulled the blue cape more closely round her as she walked briskly across the quad. The wind whistled through this ancient forecourt, reputed to be haunted, and no one chose to linger there long after dark. She had been walking with her head down against the cold but, suddenly looking up, was momentarily dazzled by a pair of brilliant headlights which seemed to have appeared from nowhere.

The car approached fast and noiselessly. For a few seconds Dido was rooted to the spot like a rabbit mesmerised by the glare, and then with horror she realised the driver either had not seen her or was intent on running her down. She leapt onto the narrow wall that enclosed a few shrubs as the enormous car swished by. In that split second of fear and evasion, her brain was clearly imprinted with the image of a black Rolls-Royce and a shadowy figure at the wheel, a proud bearing, profile like steel, eyes straight ahead.

'Damn arrogant road hog!' she expostulated. She felt

her fabled redhead's temper rising as she turned to follow him and run down the alley that led back to the quad, but her tiredness got the better of her. 'He's probably one of our famous surgeons who like to keep themselves in work,' she muttered to herself, although wondering why she had not seen that distinctive black limousine in the consultants' car park before.

She hurried out onto the main road that led to the flat. Her anger had warmed her up. In minutes she was home.

'Di, is that you?' Millie walked from the kitchen, bringing interesting cooking smells with her. 'It's my turn to make supper, and I'm experimenting,' she announced, running her hands through her short curly hair.

Dido had liked Millie from their first meeting in their student days. She was practical and humorous and unfailingly loyal, her best friend. But how different they were. They stood together in the hall as Dido took off her cape and nurse's cap. She unpinned her hair and shook out the cascade of reddish gold that waved round her face and down over her shoulders like a Botticelli angel. She unclasped the silver hands that formed the buckle on her broad blue belt and slipped off her shoes.

'That's better!' she sighed, her pale, heart-shaped face breaking into a smile which made her eyes look even more cat-like and her full lips part over small, milk-white teeth.

Millie put a plate of stew in front of Dido, then, looking down at the brilliant yellow food she explained. 'It's chicken in saffron. I was given a packet of saffron by a grateful patient today.'

'Patients can be very generous,' Dido agreed. 'In my short career, I've had everything from a bottle of the hard stuff through pounds of choccies to revealing underwear!'

Both girls laughed. They were used to being the focus of patients' fantasies, particularly in the men's wards.

'How was Men's Medical today?' Millie enquired.

'Oh, rather quiet actually. Another stroke came in—oh, and a really nice looking young man with a pneumothorax.'

'Isn't it odd that most cases of collapsed lung are in young athletic men?' Millie mused in between mouthfuls.

'Well, this poor young man had to put up with Russell making a meal of getting the chest drain in. I was holding the patient's hand and I don't think King Kong could have gripped me harder!' Dido turned back to the stew with relish. 'This is really good, Millie.'

'Is that buffoon Russell Brady still house physician on your firm?' Millie looked up as she spoke.

'Unfortunately yes. He's so arrogant and conceited but we seem to be stuck with him. Of course, Frank Berenson, our SR, is a quite different kettle of fish. He's sweet-tempered, lovely to the patients and jolly clever too. He's been doing the consultant locum these last three months while the powers that be decide on who should succeed old Carruthers. It was really tough on Frank that they didn't appoint him and brought in some hot-shot from St Cecilia's instead. He's due to meet us all tomorrow, I think.'

'Oh dear. Pity you. Benny's consultants are bad enough, but St Cecilia's are renowned for having their noses nearest to God!'

Dido laughed. Millie was doing her stint in Cardio-thoracics and had had enough of the famous surgeon who headed their firm. 'Don't be so cynical, he might be a delight,' she said, still laughing.

'Chance would be a fine thing,' Millie said darkly.

Millie had cooked and so it was Dido's turn to wash up. With her hands in the hot suds she contemplated the last two years of her career. She had been trained at St Benedict's, one of the world's leading teaching hospitals, and had enjoyed working in the heart of the City of London after growing up on a remote Wiltshire farm. Ever since she was a little girl, tending to her dolls and then her younger sister, Dido had wanted to be a nurse. She had even turned down a place at London University because she was so impatient to get on with her training.

On the whole it had lived up to her expectations. But the social life had been disappointing. Millie had acerbicly warned her when she arrived, dewy-eyed from the country, 'Love affairs with doctors are doomed. The students are sex-mad, the housemen are dog-tired and the consultants are god-almighty and hardly acknowledge your existence—except as a pair of hands doing their bidding.'

Dido looked up from her chore. 'Millie, you know you were right, when you first warned me about falling in love with doctors.'

Millie looked surprised and then smiled. 'Ah yes, I remember. Well you looked so green and shiny-new I felt I ought to arm you a little. Not that it did much good!'

'Oh, it did you know! I just had to learn my own lessons, that's all.' Dido smiled but the hurt of betrayal was still in her heart. She had fallen head over heels for the handsomest final year student, a wild, swashbuckling type who dallied with her for a few months and then left for pastures new. She had been really dazzled by him, but more hurtful than the loss of love was discovering him in the arms of a so-called friend before she knew that the affair was over. Dido still winced at the humiliation of it.

'Well, I've decided that I'm here to work. No more medical romances. I'll wait for Mr Right to come along—and it won't be in the hospital,' Dido announced.

'Don't be so sure, Di.' Millie shook her head wisely.

'Oh, you sound like the wise old woman of the mountain!' Dido threw the dishcloth at her friend, 'Here, come and help me dry these . . .'

Millie bent to pick up the cloth and noticed the muddy splashes up her friend's skirt and stockings. 'You look as if you've been playing rugger with the first years,' she said.

'What, this?' Dido looked down. 'I was practically run over by a big black Rolls that turned into the hospital quad. I don't know who was driving but he obviously didn't like me!'

'Probably come for one of the private patients,' Millie said reflectively as she dried the glasses and put them away.

The next morning dawned cold and crisp. Just two months until Christmas, Dido realised with a jolt. She had not begun to buy presents or even think what she might be doing for the holiday. She was always so busy it took all her energy to get through each day, leaving little time for planning ahead. She dressed slowly. Over her white underwear she slipped a snowy white silk and lace petticoat her godmother had bought her in Paris. It was a joy to wear, cool and slippery against her skin. Over that went the crisp blue and white striped cotton dress which she wore to just below the knee, showing off her long slim legs. That was belted by a broad blue belt with a lovely art nouveau silver buckle she had bought as a present to herself when she became Staff Nurse Alexander.

Then she had to do her hair. Keeping that under control for work was a problem. She brushed the Titian mass until it shone and then twisted it into a soft knot at the nape of her neck. Tendrils which escaped had to be pinned back and the starched white hat secured on top. She looked really quite businesslike with her hair all off her face, but her high cheekbones and tortoise-shell eyes seemed all the more noticeable.

Dido looked forward to the day ahead. She enjoyed Men's Medical; the less ill patients could be jolly and good for a laugh, and the seriously ill ones really needed devoted nursing, something that she was good at and found extremely rewarding, however heart-breaking it sometimes could be.

'Are you ready?' she called to Millie. They usually walked together to the hospital, although after tomorrow she would be going on duty as her friend came off.

The streets were full of early morning traffic, engines revving, horns sounding, exhausts steaming. When Dido and Millie turned in through the gates of the ancient St Benedict's it was like entering a sanctuary. The way a great hospital ought to be. The quad looked quite different in the early morning sun, the flower-beds spruce, the circular fish pond made a mirror by the glancing light.

Inside the main doors the familiar smell of ether and disinfectant and the constant warmth cocooned the doctors, nurses and patients alike from the outside world. Millie headed for the Cardiothoracic wing and Dido ran up the two flights of stairs to Millington, the men's medical ward she had been working on for two months.

Night Staff Anne Bradshaw was sitting at the desk, her blonde head bent as she wrote notes in the Kardex. Her face looked tired as, glancing up, she saw Dido.

'Ah, Di. I'm pleased to see you early. We've had quite a night and the new consultant is due to introduce himself this afternoon. I'm leaving you with quite a bit to do, I'm afraid.'

Dido bent over her shoulder. 'Who's new?'

'Well, there's an overdose, Mr Doone over in bed five. He's twenty and used aspirin, so we stomach-pumped and think he'll be OK. Then we had a sub-arachnoid haemorrhage, over there in bed eight, Mr Jameson. He's thirty-six, father of four. Apparently while he was watching telly last night, his wife tells us, he had a sudden blinding headache, then vomited, collapsed and slipped into a coma. He came in like this at eleven thirty. We gave him a lumbar puncture just to confirm the diagnosis and now have to wait for him to wake up. Then the neuosurgeons will get to work, ship him off for a cerebral angio and decide on treatment from that. We think it's left-sided, so at least he'll be able to speak.'

Dido took the notes and read them carefully; the poor man would need a lot of nursing. 'How's bed two, our Mr Fuller with the spontaneous pneumothorax?' As she spoke, Dido looked across at the fair-headed young man who was sitting up, reading a book and with a tube sticking from his chest leading to a large glass bottle under the bed. 'I've never had to treat a collapsed lung before,' she mused.

'Luckily it was the closed type, but it was quite a large pneumothorax so we've had to re-expand the lung by drawing the air from the pleural cavity with a catheter attached to that water-seal bottle that you see. Don't, whatever you do, pick it up.'

'Why not?' Dido asked, interested.

'Because then the water drains back into the poor patient's chest.'

'Oh lord! He looks full of beans, is he breathing normally?'

'Yes, he's recovered very well. But he's been written up for a portable chest X-ray this morning.' Staff Nurse Bradshaw stood up slowly, smoothed her skirt and tidied the desk. She was going home to sleep, having had her last night duty for a few weeks.

Sister was off sick, so Dido would be in charge of the ward that day and then start her 'nights' the following evening. The senior registrar was due in about a quarter of an hour and he and the house physician would do the ward round.

Frank Berenson had been locum for the consultant physician post for so long now, Dido knew he would find it hard to have a boss again. Specially a hot-shot brought in from St Cecilia's. She wondered how bitter he felt at being overlooked for the post. She liked him and thought him an excellent physician but had never felt any romantic stirrings, although she knew that he harboured a fondness for her. Perhaps she was proof against falling in love again, doctor or no?

There was certainly no chance of her ever falling in love with Russell Brady, the house physician, Dido thought to herself. He was so sure of himself, so condescending to her and the other nurses. He loved lording it and cared too much about his own ego and the brilliance of his diagnoses to be a good doctor. He needed to learn a little humility before he made the grade as a true physician, and Dido wondered what his come-uppance would be.

The nurses had finished with bedpans and temperatures and blood pressure. She glanced quickly round the ward. It looked bright and neatly cheerful. Everyone was in bed awaiting the doctors' round, bedspreads folded back, sheets smoothed and tucked in tight. The flowers in vases, never so profuse as on the women's wards, added brilliant dashes of colour in the pale winter sun.

Everything was as a well run hospital should be. Dido was just collecting up the notes and slipping them into the trolley when Dr Berenson and Dr Brady walked onto the ward.

'Last time before the Big Chief takes over, eh, Staff Nurse?' Frank Berenson said as he walked up to Dido's desk. 'Well, what have you got for us today?'

'Two new admissions, otherwise just as yesterday,' she said, leading the way to the first patient. 'No students today?' she enquired.

'No, they'll do tomorrow's round with Dr Dauntcey.' When Dido looked puzzled he added, 'Our new consultant. Didn't you know his name? It's James Dauntcey. Rumour has it he's *Sir* James, but doesn't use his title. It's OK for the rich and famous amongst us,' he added with a wry smile.

'Well, we're not at all impressed, title or not. We all wanted you to get the job,' Dido said warmly, touching his arm. Dr Berenson looked down at her with a sweet expression in his eyes which warmed to something more, but before he could speak Dr Brady accidentally kicked the drainage bottle attached to the tube from Mr Fuller's chest. Not surprisingly the poor young man cried out and Dido and Dr Berenson were immediately at his side, examining the catheter to make sure it had not come adrift.

'Are you all right, Henry?' Dr Berenson put his hand on the patient's arm.

'I'm OK thanks, Doc,' he swallowed.

'I *am* sorry,' Dr Brady muttered, looking down with embarrassment at his notes.

Dido examined the water-seal bottle, taking care not to pick it up, and was pleased to see that all was well.

'It won't be long before he's discharged if he goes on like this, Doctor?' she said, looking up at Dr Berenson who was comparing 'before' and 'after' X-rays.

He nodded. 'Yes, I'm very pleased. I need to see another X-ray though. One's booked for this morning isn't it, Staff? I'd like to see this lung completely re-inflated before we can set discharge dates.'

Dido led the way to Mr Jameson, her most critically ill patient. Dr Russell Brady caught up with her. 'Di, are you going to be here this evening when Sir James introduces himself?'

'Of course. I'll still be on duty.'

'Well, I've heard he's a stickler for punctuality, very demanding of his staff. He'll do anything for his patients but expects his staff to work until they drop. I hope you'll have all your nurses on their toes.' Dido ignored him. Her nurses were efficient and caring and as far as she could see could not be faulted, even by the most pedantic consultant.

They were standing at the foot of Mr Jameson's bed. He lay there pale, his eyes closed and with a drip running into his arm.

'Sub-arachnoid haemorrhage. He came in last night, in coma. We're turning him every two hours and giving him mouth care and taking blood pressure. It's high, I'm afraid, but I suppose it's what you'd expect.'

'Well done, Staff. I'd like him to have chest physio too, don't want him getting pneumonia. Now, we have to do something about this blood pressure. I suppose he's neglected it for years.' Dr Berenson stood looking down at the prone form in the neatly made bed. 'Poor devil. What a thing to hit you out of the blue. Is he married? Children?'

'Yes, he has four children. His wife is coming in as soon as she's got them off to school.' Dido could imagine what such a sudden tragedy could do to a young family.

'Let's tackle the blood pressure at least. I think ten milligrams of Hydralazine intra-muscularly every four hours, Staff.'

Dr Brady, who had kept unusually quiet during this discussion, dug his hands deep in the pockets of his white coat and cleared his throat. Dido knew he was going to make some sort of objection.

'Dr Berenson, I would have thought Diazoxide a better choice for this chap's blood pressure, given the circumstances.' Frank Berenson looked up from writing his notes, only the slight tightness of his lips betraying his irritation.

'Thank you, Dr Brady, but I think my assessment of the circumstances is perfectly thorough. Hydralazine it is, thank you, Staff.'

They moved on to the next patient, Dido wheeling the trolley with the notes, her figure trim in the crisp uniform and her hair almost under control, only a few tendrils having escaped to curl round her face like spun gold. Frank Berenson thought her the best nurse he had ever worked with. Highly intelligent, she could be trusted with the most complex jobs. She was watchful and would always know when a change in a patient's condition was cause for concern.

She also had the rare gift of making every one of her patients feel special and, however busy she was, they would never feel she did not have time to sit with them and hear their worries or answer their questions. And then there was her beauty. From the moment that she had walked on to the ward, poor Frank Berenson had been smitten by her pale, heart-shaped face, those extraordinary cat's eyes that seemed to shine golden in the sun, and her hair—the glory of which he could only imagine. He longed to pull the pins from the knot and see her tresses come tumbling down in a red-gold cascade. His reverie was interrupted by Dido's voice.

'This is Mr Doone, our other new admission. He took an overdose of aspirin, but he seems to be coming through.' She had just seen, out of the corner of her eye, her newest nurse struggling with a patient at the far side of the ward. 'Would you excuse me a moment?' she said, smiling up at the two doctors whose heads were together as they read Mr Doone's notes.

Dido was strict but fair with the young nurses under her control. She remembered when she was a new young nurse how important it was that your superiors were approachable and supportive, even while expecting the highest standards. She walked quickly up to the far end of the ward where a student nurse, Liz Stevenson, was still remonstrating with a young man who had been admitted the previous day for observation and tests.

'What's wrong, Nurse?' Dido asked calmly.

'It's Mr Stiller, Staff. He's insisting on going for a walk to see his friend in the next ward. I've told him he has to wait until after the doctors' ward round.' Dido was standing on the other side of the patient, who was complaining at having to wait so long.

'I'm sorry, Mr Stiller, Nurse Stevenson is right. You have to wait until Dr Berenson has seen you.' She placed a firm hand on his shoulder and pressed him back on to the pillows. He became more belligerent.

'I don't want to stay. There's nothing wrong with me!' His voice rose in indignation and everyone's eyes turned to watch how the pretty staff nurse would deal with this.

'That's just what we hope we'll find—that there's nothing wrong with you. But in the meantime you must stay here and abide by our rules, Mr Stiller.' Dido's voice was quiet and controlled compared to his loud blustering. Out of the corner of her eye she saw Dr Berenson begin to walk down to the bed and come to her aid. The patient threw off her hand angrily.

'Well, I don't have to stay. I want to discharge myself!' Dido's patience was wearing thin and she wanted to deal with the problem without Dr Berenson's assistance. She felt it was a kind of test case of her authority on the ward.

She put both hands on Mr Stiller's shoulders and suddenly realised how afraid he was, he was shaking so. Looking intently into his eyes, she spoke in a slow, measured tone.

'You can certainly discharge yourself right now if you wish, but I think it is in your interests, more than ours, that you stay. You want to put your mind at rest, don't you? You want to know what this weakness in your left arm means and what we can do for you?' Mr Stiller did not speak but nodded his head glumly.

'Good. Then when Dr Berenson has seen you, of course you can go and see your friend.'

'Thank you, Staff Nurse,' the young man said quietly, 'and I'm sorry for making such a fuss.'

'That's fine, Mr Stiller. I do understand.' Dido smiled one of the warm smiles which made her such a favourite with her patients. She turned back to Dr Berenson and the ward round.

'Well done, Di,' Dr Berenson said as she approached. 'He's a big guy and I thought that if it came to fisticuffs you might be rather outclassed. But I see that I needn't have worried.'

'I was rather hoping for a fight. It would have enlivened the day no end. *Beautiful Staff Nurse Floors Young Male Patient*—I can just see the headline in the student newspaper!' Dr Brady rubbed his hands. Dido felt even Frank Berenson's light-heartedness was slightly inappropriate.

'I suddenly realised how frightened the poor man is. *He's* afraid it's MS and *we're* afraid it's MS. I quite understand why he'd rather run away and discharge himself until the next attack. Still, I think he'll stay now.'

Dido drew the curtains around the bed of her over-dose patient, Mr Doone, who was showing signs of waking. She walked to his side and took his hand, brushing his hair off his forehead as he opened his eyes and looked around himself in a dazed way.

'Hello, Mr Doone. I'm Staff Nurse Alexander and you're in St Benedict's. You're going to be all right,' she said in a calm and friendly voice.

'And I'm Dr Berenson and this is Dr Brady. Are you well enough to answer a few questions about what happened?' Frank Berenson sat on the bed and talked to the patient in a caring and uncondescending way.

As Dido watched she thought how good it had been working with him, for they approached medicine in the same way. She felt sisterly and grateful towards him for teaching her so much about a career that she really loved. How were things going to change, she wondered, when this new consultant took over?

As the calibre and character of a headmaster so affected the atmosphere and relationships in a school, so the attitude and personality of a consultant affected in subtle and far-reaching ways the efficiency and happiness of his firm. Dido knew that she was not alone in waiting in trepidation to be introduced to the mysterious Dr Dauntcey; everyone from Frank Berenson down to young Lizzie Stevenson was curious and not a little anxious about how his arrival would affect their lives.

With the ward round over, Dido thought she would take an early lunch and so have more time to sort out the ward and deal with any emergencies before the scheduled five o'clock meeting with the new consultant. It was important to get off on the right foot in her professional relationship with her boss and she wanted everything to be dealt with and in its place when he arrived.

She selected a chicken salad from the canteen buffet and was relieved to see Millie and another friend waving her over to a seat on their table by the windows. She felt in need of a chatty, relaxed lunch-break.

'You look tired. A morning of dramas?' Millie enquired.

'Not exactly. We've been quite busy—we've got a sub-arachnoid who needs a lot of nursing. But really I think we're all a bit on edge about the arrival of our new boss.'

'Oh, don't worry about that,' Mary, the staff nurse from Intensive Care, chipped in. 'I did my training at St Cecilia's and James Dauntcey is meant to be very good. Difficult but good—and heart-throbbingly good-looking, into the bargain,' she added with a wink.

Millie leant forward. 'Forget work, Di. There's a big

party tomorrow night, a Halloween one. The final-years are giving it at that great barn-like flat one of them owns in City Road. I think it's number twenty-six. Anyway, everyone will be there. Do come.'

'Well, I shouldn't. I start "nights" tomorrow. But I haven't been to a party for ages, so I might. Let's take a rain-check tonight after work.' Dido remembered her new silk trousers and white silk tuxedo which made her feel so good when she wore them, or alternatively that silver 'flapper' dress. They were just the sort of glamorous clothes that she enjoyed as a contrast to the businesslike simplicity of her uniform.

The three staff nurses finished the meal chatting about their patients, the holidays they planned and their boyfriends. Dido did not join in on the last discussion, not wanting to have to explain again why she thought hospital romances did not work, for her at least. She excused herself.

'Bye, Mary. Millie, I'll be home a bit later than usual, see you then.'

She walked quickly back to the ward through familiar warm corridors, past hurrying nurses and doctors, most of whom she recognised and greeted with a smile or a, 'Good afternoon.' Dido thought of how much she liked her work. She enjoyed the responsibility and sense that she could really help people get well again, or at least come to terms with their illnesses.

St Benedict's was an ancient and venerable institution with much excellent pioneering medicine being practised there, but Dido felt it was her job not only to administer the best treatments, but to make sure that the patients' needs were anticipated and catered for at all times. She believed that a happy, informed patient was half-way to being a cured patient.

She entered Millington, her own ward, and noticed with pleasure how clean and bright it looked. These old hospitals had many disadvantages, but the wards were big and airy with great tall windows on two sides letting in a flood of light. Today the winter sun spread shafts of pale gold on the beds and some of her patients were just dozing in its warmth like contented cats.

She went quickly to check on Mr Jameson. He was still in coma and had just had his two-hourly turning and a new drip bag put up. Dido thought he looked a little less death-like and took his hand and stroked it, talking encouragingly to him.

His wife had visited that morning and had seemed stunned by the tragedy that had befallen her family without warning. Dido had explained that when her husband regained consciousness he would be given a cerebral angiogram, when a dye would be injected into the blood-vessels in the brain via the carotid artery in his neck. And then with a series of X-rays the neuro-surgeons would be able to locate the bleeding. If an operation were possible, they would tie off the weak blood-vessel that was causing all the trouble.

Mrs Jameson had wanted to know if her husband would be paralysed and Dido could honestly only say that everyone would have to wait and see. But in her heart she knew that it was most unlikely that he would recover fully.

The afternoon passed quickly in the routine of nursing care; drug administration, note-writing, temperature and blood pressure recording, charting input and output of fluid, talking to the patients, making them comfort-able, adjusting drips, dressing wounds and removing stitches. Suddenly it was a quarter to five and Dido felt she had not stopped once since lunch, even to draw breath. The meeting was to be held in Sister's office so she walked briskly down the ward to the small room near the entrance doors, picking up a vase of chrysanthemums from the main desk to brighten things up a bit.

It was already dusk outside and the lights in the ward were on. Dido straightened the books and files in the office and put coffee and water into the coffee-making machine, a generous present from an old patient. Everything was now as ready as it would ever be and she strolled back into her ward, called her nurses and reminded them of the meeting and the need for punctuality.

Just as they were assembling, Nurse Stevenson rushed up and said that Mr Doone, the overdose patient, was threatening to discharge himself. He was very disturbed and weeping, she reported.

'You go ahead then, all of you, and tell Dr Berenson I will be along soon. Nurse Stevenson, will you pour out the coffee when Dr Dauntcey arrives? It should be done by now.'

Dido walked smartly up the ward to where muffled sobs were coming from Mr Doone's bed, and drew the curtains. She gently pulled down the sheet and looked into a pair of red-rimmed eyes. Taking his hand, Dido sat down on the chair beside his bed.

'Now, tell me, what's upsetting you?' she asked calmly. The young man was desperate to talk and his life story tumbled out, at times almost incoherent, at times reducing him to tears again. Dido knew that she would be late for the meeting but her first priority was to make this patient feel a little less isolated and misunderstood.

She listened intently to him, answering him when he asked questions and making a mental note to ring up his girlfriend, whom he wanted to see very badly. When his story was finished he seemed relieved and more relaxed and Dido stood up, still holding his hand, and asked him if he was feeling better.

He nodded and she added,

'We haven't forgotten you. The psychiatrist is going to come and talk to you tomorrow. You'll like her, she's very good and sympathetic, you can tell her everything. I think she'll help you sort out your feelings a bit more.'

Mr Doone nodded again. 'Thanks for being so patient,' he said. 'I feel as if a cloud of confusion has been blown away.' And for the first time, Staff Nurse Alexander saw him smile.

She hurried up to Sister's room, suddenly feeling the nervousness she had been too busy to allow to surface before. The lights were on and through the glass partition she could see the white caps of her nurses, Dr Brady and Dr Berenson's white coats and the smart dark suit which must belong to the new consultant.

As she opened the door all eyes turned towards her and Dido felt her colour rise. One pair of eyes, so blue and glittering, held her gaze and stopped her in her tracks.

'Sir, this is Staff Nurse Alexander.' Dr Berenson's mild voice hardly penetrated her consciousness as she stood transfixed by the intensity of Dr Dauntcey's look.

'On my ward, punctuality is of utmost importance if we are to run an efficient firm.' His voice was cold and disapproving. Immediately the spell of his gaze was broken and Dido was aware that her temper was rising.

How dare he censure her in front of her staff! How dare he not even bother to enquire why she was late! What arrogance!

Before she could stop herself she said, 'Well, on my ward, the patients come first, Dr Dauntcey.'

He had been talking to Frank Berenson and now his gaze returned to Dido's face. '*Your* ward, Staff Nurse? Where's Sister?' Dido could not trust herself to speak and resolutely bit her tongue, grateful that Frank interjected.

'Sister's off sick and Di—Staff Nurse Alexander—has been running the ward, and making a very good job of it too.' Dido managed a tight smile and got a wink in return from Dr Berenson. One of the nurses handed her a cup of coffee and she took the opportunity of drinking it to slowly regain her composure.

She felt empty and miserable and suddenly very tired. She had badly wanted to make a good impression. She had been in charge of the ward for the last week and it had been a demanding job and she knew she had done it well. But just when she had wanted her efficiency and intelligence to be most noticed, when their new consultant was being introduced to the ward, she had been branded a disorganised and rude young woman instead. The mortification made Dido's cheeks burn.

Still, despite her disappointment and anger, she could not help being slightly curious about their new boss. Dr Dauntcey was discussing something with Frank Berenson and Dido took the opportunity to try and assess from his looks what he would be like to work with.

She had to admit grudgingly that he was the most handsome man she had ever seen, with the sort of dark good looks that belonged more to a movie star than a hard-working consultant in a central London teaching hospital. Yet there was a shadow, a guardedness in his face that Dido could not fathom.

But the mark of sorrow on his face was fleeting and barely discernible. To the rest of the world he looked tall and lean in his immaculately fitting dark suit, with a tenseness and poise which suggested the reserved strength of an athlete. Dido was sure that he played squash or ran in his spare time. Certainly the outer curve of his powerful thigh muscles could be seen as he elegantly crossed one leg over the other.

Then, as he turned further round to answer a query from Dr Brady, she saw his distinctive profile. Dido gave a little gasp. Its straightness, the line of his narrow nose and full lips, the set of the jaw, all stirred her memory. That was it! He was the driver of the car which had almost run her down in the quad last night! Dido's heart sank. She could not have got off to a worse start.

There was a stir in the room as Dr Dauntcey stood up and smiled,

'Thank you for coming to this informal meeting. I look forward very much to our association and I'm sure it will be a happy and successful one. I'll be here tomorrow at ten for the ward round and will see you all then.' Without meeting Dido's eyes he walked out of the room, followed by Frank and Russell Brady.

Dido was just thankful that tomorrow was her day off before night duty began and she therefore would not have to endure making a fool of herself on the consultant's ward round in the morning.

CHAPTER TWO

DIDO opened the door of the flat and threw herself into the nearest chair. She called out, hoping Millie would answer. Tonight of all nights she felt like a chat with her good-humoured friend, but only silence greeted her call. Dido eased her feet out of her shoes and leant her head back against the chair.

She tried to empty her mind of the events of the last two hours. She knew there was nothing to be gained by brooding. But try as she might, the humiliating scene in Sister's office ran through her head repeatedly in vivid Technicolor with wrap-around sound. The unfairness of it! If only she had kept her cool and explained. She admonished herself for her hot-headedness. Then with relief she heard Millie's distinctive footsteps clattering up the stairs, the rattle of her key in the lock and her flushed face and wildly unruly hair appeared round the door.

'Hello, Di, you looked bushed!' she said as she threw her shoulder-bag down in the hall. Millie rang her fingers through her hair in characteristic fashion and the curls settled into a less dishevelled style. 'I know, you could do with a cup of tea,' she said, and without waiting for an answer walked through to the kitchen.

That was why she was such a special friend, Dido thought to herself. She would always know when one needed support and would cheerfully offer it without hesitation or reproach. Dido closed her eyes and did not open them again until she felt the cool rim of a saucer being put into her hands.

'Oh, Millie! What a treat. It's just what I need.'

'Well, tell me about the dreaded consultant then.' She knew Dido's exhaustion was almost certainly due to the extra work preparing the ward for her new chief and she was curious to hear first impressions of him.

'What's there to tell?' Dido's voice was tired. 'All I know is I blotted my copybook by being late for the meeting and he's blotted his by being insufferably rude and overbearing. So it doesn't bode too well for our future working relationship.' She looked dispiritedly at her friend.

'Don't let it get you down, Di. First impressions are often misleading. You're just overworked and under-appreciated, it's a common nursing complaint. Look, get to bed early and then come to the medic's Halloween party with me tomorrow night.' Millie was leaning forward enthusiastically. 'Come on, say you will. It will do you good to let your hair down.'

At that moment, Dido could not think of anything that she felt less like doing than going to a rowdy, high-spirited student party, but she knew that having caught up on some sleep she would feel differently tomorrow.

'OK. But do we have to dress up? I don't know what I could wear.'

The tea had revived Dido and the sparkle was back in her eyes.

'It's a sort of fancy-dress affair. I know, why don't you wear that fantastic silver 'twenties' dress you bought in the market? With your hair down you could go as a nymph or an angel, quite a change from all the witches and warlocks there'll be gadding about.'

Dido was suddenly much more enthusiastic. 'Yes, and

I've got that silvery glitter stuff I bought two years ago and never used. I can dust that in my hair. It could be fun. But what'll you wear, Millie?'

Millie pulled her chair closer and giggled. 'Well, I'm going as a black cat in my leotard and tights. I've stuffed a black stocking for a tail and have a half a squash ball for my little black nose. I've stuck some cardboard ears on a headband and have got a piece of fake fur as the white patch on my chest. I'm awfully pleased with it.'

Dido laughed wholeheartedly for the first time that day. 'You'll look marvellous Millie! You're like a lucky little cat in real life—you're just giving form to your true character.'

'We'll both wow them all. So you're definitely coming? Good.' Then Millie added, 'Seeing I won't be having to cook supper tomorrow night, I'll do it tonight and give you a break. Now, finish that book you're reading or watch telly. Just forget about work and your arrogant consultant for one night, at least.'

Dido gathered up her things and smiled broadly at her friend. 'Thanks, Millie. You've made me feel normal again.'

The next morning Dido woke up at six-thirty as usual and then, remembering it was her day off, turned over and slipped back into luxurious sleep. It was ten o'clock before she surfaced again and she set about having a long bath, washing her hair, painting her toenails, all in leisurely preparation for the party tonight.

Dressed in a pair of jeans and an old shirt she decided to get a few chores round the flat done before indulging herself with the romantic novel she was already half-way through and longing to finish. Dido managed to dispel the previous day's work and humiliation from her mind and had at last settled down for a good read when the telephone rang.

Wondering who, apart from Millie, knew anyone would be there at this time of day, she picked up the receiver. Pips were followed by a man's voice.

'Hello, is that you Di?' She immediately recognised Frank Berenson's intonation and was surprised at how pleased she was to hear his voice.

'Hello, Frank,' she said warmly.

'Sorry to bother you on your day off, but I wondered if you were going to the party tonight?'

'Yes. Millie's persuaded me to. It should be fun.'

'Oh good. I also rang to tell you not to take to heart last evening's confrontation with the devilish Dr D! He has a reputation for being a stickler and I think you held your own very well.' He chuckled and Dido immediately felt more cheered.

'Well, thank you for sticking up for me.'

'Anytime you need some support you can rely on me,' he answered with a more serious inflexion in his voice. Dido knew he wanted to say more, but she was not ready yet to hear it. She quickly brought the conversation to a close.

'Thanks for ringing, Frank. I look forward to seeing you tonight.'

'Can I pick you up in my jalopy?' he interjected quickly.

'That would be lovely, but it'd have to be Millie as well. We're going together.'

'Fine. I'll pick you up at nine. See you then.'

Dido returned to her book with a sigh. Sweet, nice Frank, he was such a good friend. Why could she feel nothing more for him than friendship? It had been almost a year now since she had felt any romantic feelings for anybody. Dido wondered bleakly if she had not put her heart somehow into permanent cold storage.

Slowly she started to roll strands of her hair in rags, tying them how her grandmother had taught her, to make the natural wave more ruly. She was enjoying preparing for this party instead of the usual rush that followed a late return from work. Soon her head was covered with parcels of golden hair interleaved and tied with ribbons of white sheeting, It looks quite fetching as it is, Dido mused to herself.

And then an unexpected melancholy descended upon her. If only she was going to this trouble for someone special who would gaze at her with love and admiration, with naked passion in his eyes. She was staring intently at her reflection in the mirror and her tortoise-shell eyes stared back. They looked so sad Dido felt for a moment on the edge of a deluge of self-pity. But she checked herself and turned away.

'You're expecting life to be a fairy-tale,' she scolded herself aloud. 'Handsome princes do not gallop out of the mist and sweep you away!' As she marvelled at her naivety she reminded herself of all her blessings; a good, responsible job she enjoyed, loving parents, good friends, her health and good looks. She began to feel ashamed at her attack of self-pity.

Millie would be home soon after a hard day on the ward and Dido thought with gratitude of her best friend's unfailing good nature. They would not be feeling like a full supper tonight so she decided to go and buy a melon and a big bunch of grapes from the corner greengrocer as a treat. Tying a headscarf over her rag-doll hair, she rushed out. It was already growing dark as she left the shop with her purchases. Suddenly she caught sight of Millie in her navy cape just turning the corner ahead.

'Millie!' she called, and then broke into a jog. 'I've just bought us a melon for tea. Let's be greedy and have half each.' Millie looked pale and very tired and Dido turned to look at her with concern. 'Are you all right? You look whacked.'

Millie smiled rather wanly. 'Yes, I'm OK. We've just had a death and it shook us all. I'll get over it.'

'Do you want to talk?' Dido enquired quietly as she walked along beside her.

'There's nothing much to it. It's just he was young, about twenty-five and such a happy-go-lucky sort of person. So kind to other patients on the ward, too. He was in for a double valve repair. That went all right, but then we couldn't get him off bypass. It does seem such a waste of life, that's all.'

They had arrived back at the front door of the converted Victorian house whose top floor comprised their flat.

'Would you rather give the party tonight a miss? I'll stay and keep you company if you like.' Dido managed to hide her disappointment at the prospect.

'Oh no. I'll recover. All I need is a cup of tea. And half a melon,' Millie added with a pale attempt at a smile.

'I'm glad. At least we'll have a lift. Frank Berenson, the SR on my ward, is coming to pick us up at nine.' They climbed the stairs together and Dido went straight through to the kitchen to put the kettle on to make the tea.

It was five minutes before nine o'clock and Dido was just dusting the silver glitter into her hair when the doorbell rang. Millie was already fully dressed, whiskered and tailed, and she uncurled from her seat by the gas fire in a thoroughly cat-like way.

'I'll get it. You finish the coiffure.'

Dido looked at herself critically. The dress was spectacular, silver lace and sequins on net, and the shape, beautifully cut and seamed, skimmed over her body so becomingly that her small waist seemed even narrower and her curves more curvaceous.

'I look more like a thirties screen goddess than an angel, but never mind,' she told herself.

Dido was pleased, too, with her hair. The rags had given more shape and form to the mass of red-gold and it cascaded round her face and down her back like a fine silken mane. The silver dress seemed to add an extra translucency to her skin and her speckled eyes appeared darker and more mysterious than ever. Dido felt surprised and gratified that she could look so striking when she tried.

She turned as she heard Millie and Frank's voices at the door.

'Hello!' Frank called out and then stopped, a slightly stunned expression on his face. He let his breath out in a sigh and said, 'Di, you look fantastic! Who would have thought efficient, giant-slaying Staff Nurse Alexander could look so glamorous!'

Dido had to laugh, not least because Frank was dressed as a gorilla and had his rubber mask in his hand. 'What about Millie? Isn't she the most endearing witch's cat?'

Millie was purring and stalking round the room on tiptoe.

'Yes. I've already told her I'd give her a warm hearth and a saucer of milk any day,' Frank said with a grin. Then he added, 'Come on girls, we're late already.' He led the way down to the street where his old Alfa Romeo sports car was parked askew at the kerb.

They could hear the party before they actually saw it. The sound of pop music, talk and laughter floated down the street as they approached. Dido suddenly felt nervous. It was a much bigger affair than she had expected. Frank pushed open the door and held it back for Dido and Millie to enter.

For a moment Dido stood in the light, blinking at the sight that met her eyes. The cavernous room was dimly lit with flickering candles in brackets on the wall. There were small pumpkin-lights on the tables set around the edges, and the centre of the room was filled with dancing, cavorting witches, wizards, fairies, hobgoblins, hairy animals and human mutations, some fleetingly recognisable as the responsible, hard-working doctors and nurses of St Benedict's.

'An angel descended into hell to save us!' Russell Brady called out from across the room, threading his way through the dancing bodies to greet them.

He was dressed unaccountably as Robin Hood, but Dido thought it was probably a good excuse for him to show off his swagger in big boots and green tights. He immediately took her hand and swung her into the throng for an energetic dance to the deafening music.

'We missed you on the ward round this morning,' he shouted through the noise. 'Dr Dauntcey kept us all on our toes. Picked up an unsuspected retinal haemorrhage in old Mr Smithers, the diabetic in bed twelve.'

'Can't you talk about anything other than medicine?' Dido shouted back at him, but her words were lost in the general hubbub of voices and music. She decided to get on with dancing instead and threw herself with gusto into a bit of rock 'n' roll with Russell, as the old Elvis favourite 'Blue Suede Shoes' blared out from the speakers.

Having been her home town's champion dancer when she was sixteen, Dido realised, as she felt the music surge through her head and her body begin to flow, how much she had missed regular dancing when she moved away from home. All too soon the record was over and a slow beat tune began.

'Let's find Frank and Millie and sit this one out,' Dido said as she scanned the packed room. 'There they are! Over by the bar.'

'You two make unlikely but marvellous rockers. I knew Russell was a bit of a mover by his skilful side-stepping of night calls, but every minute it seems I'm learning new and surprising truths about you, Di.' Frank had already ordered them their drinks.

'Have you been out on the floor yet, Millie?' Dido sat down next to her friend and stretched out her legs.

'We did hoof it a bit to that last record, but I'm not in your class, Di. I never realised you were such a dancer.'

'I haven't rock 'n' rolled for ages, and I suddenly realised how much I missed it,' Dido said, sipping gratefully at the cool drink in her hand.

Frank moved away from the bar and sat down beside her. 'You would have enjoyed seeing a real professional at work this morning.'

'Who, you?' Dido looked up at him quizzically.

'No silly, James Dauntcey. He's terribly sharp. Did Russell tell you about Mr Smithers? I felt bad that I hadn't thought to check his sight before, but Dauntcey didn't make an issue of it at all.'

'How did he suspect something was wrong?' Dido was interested and would hope to be able to pick up something like that next time.

'Well, Mr Smithers was just complaining to Staff that
he couldn't see telly properly. Quick as a flash our clever
consultant called for an ophthalmascope and within a
couple of minutes had diagnosed the haemorrhage and
prescribed laser treatment, which luckily St Benedict's
can provide.'

'Which staff nurse was on duty?'

'Julie Williams. Rather ham-fisted and not terribly
bright. I'm afraid she got up the great consultant's nose a
bit. In fact he rather pointedly asked where you were.'

Dido was surprised and secretly a little gratified. She'd
show him yet that she was an exceptionally responsible
and intelligent nurse. She'd pick up some condition
everyone else had missed. She'd show the arrogant man
just what she was made of!

'Anyway, enough of work. I want to know something
about you, Dido Alexander. In the space of a few hours
I've been stunned by the beauty of your hair and your
fantastic dancing. What other revelations are you
harbouring?'

Dido laughed. Frank could hardly expect to conduct a
serious conversation sitting there in his gorilla suit with
one very hairy leg crossed over the other!

'I'm just an ordinary working girl. OK, so I've got long
hair and can dance, but that's all.'

A couple of Frank's colleagues had approached,
hoping for an introduction to Dido, but he had waved
them away with a cavalier hand. He did not want this
first real conversation with her to be interrupted or
distracted.

'What about your family?' he persisted.

'I have one younger brother and he and my parents
live in Wiltshire in the house I was brought up in.'

'Is your father a doctor?' Frank seemed hungry for

any pieces of information he could glean about her character and background.

'He was a GP but is retired now. And my mother was a nurse.' She smiled at the memory of them.

'Ah, the very best love match.' Frank put one eager hairy paw on Dido's glitter-dusted hand.

'I disagree,' she said rather more forcefully than she had meant. 'I think a nurse would be mad to fall in love with a doctor, certainly a hospital doctor.' Frank's face fell and Dido immediately felt sorry for sounding rather harsh. 'Anyway, that's how I feel about it. It's nothing personal.' And she patted his paw in a friendly way.

'Come and dance.' Frank took her elbow and steered her onto the dance floor. Millie and Russell, who had been chatting at the next table, followed.

It was impossible to be out of sorts for long, surrounded as they were by an extraordinary variety of fancy dress. Soon Dido and Frank were roaring with laughter as they recognised their colleagues in weird costumes behaving in various degrees of abandon. Dressing up as characters other than themselves seemed to give certain more formal members of the medical profession greater license to relax and be outrageous than if they had turned up in their conventional uniform of dark suits.

Dido pointed out to Frank, with a shout of laughter, the luminous skeleton suit stretched over an ample figure that was none other than Mr de Vere Thomas, the ultra-chic heart surgeon who headed the prestigious Cardiothoracic unit where Millie worked.

'Millie, look!' she called urgently to her friend, who was dancing energetically some feet away.

'Where? What?' Millie yelled over the throng.

'De Vere Thomas, over there!' Dido mouthed back at

her, and Millie's eyes followed Dido's discreetly pointing finger, a great crowing of delight escaping from her.

'Oh, this is wonderful!' she laughed, scanning the
crowd for more bizarre combinations. The music
changed to another up-beat number and Dido found
herself whisked away by Danny Evans, the registrar on
her previous ward.

'Sorry, old boy!' he bowed to Frank. 'You can't hog
the lovely Di's company. I'll return her to you later and
unharmed.' Danny was short, athletic and distinctly
hyper-active. He spun Dido into an exhaustingly fast
jive, throwing her into double loops and turns. For one
heart-stopping moment she feared he was going to pick
her up and spin her over his head.

'How're you enjoying Men's Medical?' he asked
during a brief lull in the action.

'Fine,' was all Dido had time to say.

'We all miss you,' he yelled back over the noisy refrain
of the record. Then as the song died, Frank came up to
reclaim Dido. 'Di, you're more delicious than any
woman I've ever met,' Danny said as he kissed her
appreciatively on the cheek.

Frank's face turned stonier. He had never liked
Danny and seemed to resent his claim on Dido's
attention and time. She sensed this and started to walk
back to the table where Millie sat in lively conversation
with a young man who moved off as Dido approached.

'Thanks for the dance, Danny,' she smiled in a kind
dismissal.

'You look as if you're enjoying yourself,' Millie whispered to Dido as she sat down beside her.

'I am, but are you too?' Millie had taken off her cat's
nose and whiskers and her face looked a little drawn and
rather sad.

'Yes, of course,' she said in a less than confident voice.
'I know it's silly, but I was half hoping I might meet
someone special here tonight,' she added, her words
tumbling out in an embarrassed rush.

'Oh, Millie, you will meet someone special. When the
time's ripe it'll happen.' Dido looked towards the bar
where Frank was collecting some more cool drinks. 'You
like Frank, don't you?'

'Of course. He's a really nice man. But he's not really
my type, and, anyway, he's besotted with you. Hadn't
you noticed?'

'I do know, but it makes me feel guilty that it's not
reciprocated. He's a really good friend and a jolly good
doctor, but that's all.'

Frank returned with a tray of drinks which he
proceeded to hand around. Millie leant over and whispered, 'Di, I'm afraid I'll have to go soon. It's past
twelve and I've got an early duty tomorrow. But you
stay.'

'Of course I'll come with you!' Dido was adamant. 'I
wouldn't dream of letting you go home on your own.'
Frank overheard the conversation and butted in.

'And I wouldn't dream of letting you ladies go home
on your own. I'll take you. But first, one last dance each.
Millie, do me the honour,' and he bowed in an old-
fashioned way and proffered his arm as Millie got to her
feet.

Dido sat back and watched the dancers. People had
removed their masks and animal heads and were much
more easily recognisable, yet more bizarre, their own
human heads topping strangely dressed-up bodies. Dido
sat tapping her feet, looking forward to her dance, even
though it would be the last. As the music stopped and
Millie and Frank threaded their way back through the

throng, Dido stood up, tossed her hair back from her face and took Frank's arm.

The disc jockey, who had been selecting the records and playing the occasional request, caught sight of Dido and called out, 'What can I play for the beautiful girl with the red hair?' Dido, suddenly realising that he meant her and that everyone's eyes were on her, some of the dancers clapping and calling out suggestions, could only think to ask for 'Blue Suede Shoes' again.

The familiar old classic got everyone to their feet in a great surge and as the music pounded out Dido gave herself up to the dance. Frank was a good partner, sure-footed, hardly moving his own body as he spun her to left and to right of him. Dido's dress, heavy with silver embroidery, lifted and swung out about her legs. Her hair was flying. Gradually she was aware that the floor was clearing, that other dancers had stopped and were watching her and Frank, clapping in time to the music and cheering every virtuoso move.

Frank seemed to warm to the occasion and, pulling Dido towards him at the start of a spin, said, 'When you come out of this, put your feet together and relax.' Dido knew she was in for a few pyrotechnics but she had no chance to protest.

Suddenly she was spinning and then, feet together, *whoosh*, she had been pulled towards Frank and then effortlessly catapulted between his legs. Her skirt swooped up to the top of her thighs but in that split second Dido managed to extricate herself gracefully by leaping to her feet and swinging back into the jive. A great cheering and clapping greeted this move and cries of 'Again,' led by the student doctors over by the bar.

But at that moment, inexplicably, Dido noticed one face in the sea that surrounded her, one dark-suited body among the kaleidoscope of fancy dress, one pair of cold blue, inscrutable eyes. Her unselfconscious spontaneity, her pleasure in dancing, evaporated instantly. She met his eyes again, watching intently. Were they full of disapproval or were they just dispassionate, neither recognising her as the staff nurse he had crossed swords with the previous day, nor caring who she might be?

Frank was still high on the attention and indicated he wanted to attempt the move again as a grand finale, but he realised by Dido's frantic expression that he had better not try it. Mercifully the music was fading and the dancers were returning to their partners. Frank pulled her into his arms and kissed her wetly on the neck.

'Thanks for a super time,' he said. Dido was too confused and demoralised to resist his embrace.

She turned to go back to their table and collect Millie, but her arm was taken by Danny, now rather the worse for drink.

'I want one last dance, Di,' he said with a tell-tale slur in his speech.

'No, I'm going home now, Danny,' Dido said coolly.

Frank came up behind her and added, a little unwisely, 'You're drunk, Danny. It's time you went home.'

Suddenly the shorter man launched himself at Frank, pushing him roughly in the chest, his voice rising to a shout which attracted everyone's less welcome attention.

'Don't you tell me I'm drunk! I was talking to Di, not you. You don't own her!'

Dido was cringing with embarrassment, humiliated all the more by the knowledge that Dr Dauntcey was watching all this, had seen her being frivolous and showing off on the dance floor and now being the cause of a vulgar fracas between another doctor and his own senior registrar. She just knew she had to extricate herself from the situation as cleanly and quickly as she could.

'Danny,' Dido said quietly, but her eyes, intent on his face, blazed with anger, 'I told you, I am going home. Thanks for the offer. Now let me pass.'

Through his drink-befuddled brain, Danny recognised her determination and he stood aside without a murmur. Dido looked around wildly for Millie and was relieved to see that she had already collected their coats and was beckoning from the doorway. Then she realised Frank had momentarily disappeared.

'Where's Frank?' she whispered anxiously to Millie.

'Over there, with that tall dark man.' Dido's eyes followed Millie's pointing finger and her heart, already heavy, sank into the floor. There she saw Frank and Dr Dauntcey huddled together, deep in conversation. Then, as she watched, they both glanced up, catching sight of her standing silhouetted in the doorway, her hair like flaming filaments around her pale, luminous face. Once again those eyes, so intense, so apparently disapproving, bored into hers. For Dido it was the last straw. She turned quickly and, with Millie following, rushed out into the street.

'Who's the man Frank's with?' Millie panted after her.

'Just the new consultant, Dr James Dauntcey, that's all,' said Dido wearily. How cruelly ironic it seemed that she should vow earlier to prove to that man what a reasonable and intelligent nurse she was! Well, you've blown that for good, she thought despairingly.

'Wait! Di, Millie! I'm giving you a lift home, remember! Why didn't you wait?' Frank came running down the road behind them.

'I thought you were busy with your boss,' Dido said dispiritedly.

'Oh, he just wanted a word about tomorrow's clinical meeting. Anyway, it's boss's orders to get you two girls home safely to bed.'

'What! You mean he thinks we're drunk too?' Dido's temper flared, despite her tiredness.

'Of course not. He knows Danny from St Cecilia's. He knows he's a hot-headed little Welshman. No, he just looked up as you were standing in the doorway and said, "Get that staff nurse home soon—I don't want exhausted staff on the ward."'

'Did he recognise me?' Dido asked shyly, curious despite herself.

'Well, he didn't call you by your pet name, but he knew you were a staff nurse—unless he thought you were Staff Nurse Williams with a body and a head transplant,' he added with a wicked sidelong grin.

The moment Dido got into her room she peeled off her beautiful silver dress, resisted the impulse to throw it in a heap on the floor, brushed the silver glitter from her hair and washed her face until it was squeaky clean. She wished she could as easily wash away the night's events.

Climbing wearily into bed, Dido could only welcome tomorrow night. Night duty seemed to be the only thing that would keep her out of trouble.

CHAPTER THREE

DIDO slept late. The rest of the day passed in household chores, cleaning, mending and cooking a special supper for Millie and herself to enjoy before she left for the hospital to start her night duty. She had been so busy, and careful, too, not to dwell on last night's events, that suddenly eight-thirty, the time for her departure, was near.

'Look at the time. I can't be late on my first night on!' Dido quickly started to put on her uniform and Millie collected her coat and bag for her.

'Don't worry, it's only a quarter of an hour or so to the hospital. You'll make it easily.'

Dido was twisting her hair into a loose bun and pinning her newly-laundered cap on top when she noticed that there were still silver speckles of glitter scattered in her curls. It was too late now to give them the vigorous brushing they needed. That would have to wait until tomorrow, when she came off duty.

'Thanks, Millie,' she called as she ran, fleet-footed, down the stairs and out into the street.

It was a dense, dark night, with neither stars nor the moon to relieve the blackness of the sky. Dido walked quickly through the gloom of the residential street where she lived, heading for the brightly-lit main thoroughfare ahead. She never felt afraid at night, dressed in her distinctive nurse's uniform, the noticeable white cap her badge of caring and authority.

At last, turning in through the great stone portico of

the hospital gates, she had still to walk across the dark, mysterious quad beyond. But at this time there were a number of people coming on duty or going home, and the atmosphere was familiar and friendly. Dido ran up the steps to the main door and pushed through into the warmth and brightness of hospital life. It was five minutes to nine when she walked onto Millington ward to be greeted by Staff Nurse Williams' broad, freckled face.

'Hello Di,' she greeted her with a smile. 'After that dancing display last night I'm glad to see you're still in one piece.'

Dido managed a tight smile. Ignoring the reference to events of the previous night, she took off her cape and hung it in Sister's office. She was keen to catch up on her patients' progress.

'Has it been busy today?' she asked Julie in a friendly way before tackling the important details of their change-over. 'How's Mr Jameson in bed eight? The sub-arachnoid haemorrhage.' He had been Dido's most seriously ill patient and had needed a great deal of careful nursing, what with the chest physiotherapy, mouth care, intravenous hydration and, of course, the intra-muscular Hydralazine for his blood pressure. She really hoped to hear there had been some improvement.

'He's still unconscious and I'm afraid he had a slight fever today. We're testing urine and sputum and doing a blood count to find out what organism might be causing the trouble.' Dido felt there was a depressing inevitability about it.

'How's his BP? Frank Berenson was confident that four hourly Hydralazine would do the trick.

'Yes, let's see, his blood pressure is well down. Gosh, I didn't realise it had got so out of hand! That first reading is one of the highest I've come across.' Staff

Nurse Williams' eyes widened as she looked up from her notes. 'We're also hydrating him with three litres of dextrose-saline every twenty-four hours, but then the drip was probably up before you went off duty, wasn't it, Di?'

'Has his wife been in regularly? Difficult as it must be with all those children, I do believe it can help, even when a patient's unconscious.' Dido looked across at Mr Jameson's bed and felt a real sympathy for his wife, who had seen the man she loved, the father of her children, reduced in one split second to this comatose half-life. Julie Williams' eyes followed Dido's as she answered.

'Yes, regular as clockwork. She sits by his bed talking to him, telling him about the children.' Dido looked away. She and the doctors knew that the longer he remained unconscious the less likely he was to recover at all. Even the most optimistic prognosis would be a bleak one for Mr Jameson and his family.

'I hope you've been able to discharge Mr Doone, the overdose in bed five?'

'Yes. Today. He cheered up no end after his girlfriend visited him. She said you'd rung her. Was that so?' When Dido nodded Julie continued, 'The psychiatrist came and spent some time with him, pronounced him fit and well and he went home with his girlfriend.'

'How about bed two, Mr Fuller, wasn't it? The handsome young man with the spontaneous pneumothorax.'

'He's been discharged too. The X-ray showed his lung fully expanded. We moved the tube and X-rayed him again a few hours later, as our old battle-axe sister tutor taught us all those years ago. So home he went, collected by a beautiful girl—which rather dashed the hopes among our younger, more impressionable nurses.'

Dido laughed. She well remembered how, as a

student nurse, it was so easy to get romantic about a good-looking male patient. All that professional hand-holding and caring, often through a crisis in the patient's life, created a falsely emotionally charged relationship. No harm came of it and the young nurses quickly learnt to recognise the symptoms in themselves and others.

'So we've lost two. Who's left? How about Mr Stiller, the MS suspect? Has he had a myelogram yet?' Julie flicked through the Kardex and ran her fingers down the entries under Mr Stiller's name.

'Myelogram today. That was negative, so we can't rule out MS. Some of the cerebro-spinal fluid has been sent off for analysis, but that'll take about ten days.' Dido was thoughtful, remembering the man's fear of having the disease, which he had suspected he had for the last year, finally diagnosed.

'A myelogram's an unpleasant procedure but worth it if it shows the limb weakness is due to pressure on the spinal cord rather than multiple sclerosis. What a pity we couldn't put his mind at rest. I suppose the lumbar puncture's left him with a cracking headache?'

'Dr Berenson prescribed codeine phosphate and bed-rest for at least twenty-four hours.'

The ward doors swung open and Frank Berenson strode in, his white coat flying.

'Hello, Julie, Di. I know you're talking about me. I'm just going off duty but want to give you the background on a new patient. He's on his way up, rather late in the day—I'm sorry.'

He gave Dido the man's notes—Mr Manetti, one of the market porters with alcoholic cirrhosis. 'His GP referred him for jaundice but there's a history of heavy drinking, a bottle of gin for breakfast, that sort of thing,

and there's definite liver disease. We just have to determine how serious.'

Dido shook her head. Did people realise just how
much damage they were doing to themselves? From her
side of the fence it seemed all too commonplace an urge
to self-destruction.

'You'll want to do a liver biopsy I presume?' she
looked at the notes.

'Yes, eventually, but we have to wait for the results on
the clotting properties of his blood, otherwise we could
be in real trouble.'

'What about nursing in the meantime. Something to
prevent d.t.'s?' She looked up enquiringly at Frank, only
then noticing how pale and tired he looked.

'I've written out a prescription for Heminevrin to
sedate him, and thiamine of course. Both very important. Would you call Russell in to have a look at him when
he arrives on the ward? If there's any trouble or
deterioration I can be reached at home.'

'You look really tired, Frank,' Dido said quietly,
concern in her eyes. He smiled wanly and propped
himself against her desk.

'I am. I was called out at four this morning. Haven't
stopped since. But I'm really and truly going off duty
now and I think I'll spend what's left of the evening in
bed.'

'Medicine doesn't do much for one's social life,' Dido
smiled wryly.

'You're telling me!' Frank exclaimed. 'Last night was
my first real night out for months. Most of the time I'm
catching up on lost sleep or pacing hospital corridors.
Still, last night was worth it. I had a lovely time, thanks
to you.' And Frank picked up his brief-case and pushed
his way back through the swing doors.

Julie Williams had left soon after Frank's arrival and now Dido had the ward to herself, with just Nurse Peters to help. She looked around. The television was on quietly in the corner, reading-lights were casting a soft glow and her patients sat in small groups talking or lay in bed reading. Only poor Mr Jameson lay inert in his bed, somehow seeming more shrunken than when she had last seen him.

Around his prone body was arranged the paraphernalia of modern medicine, drip stands and the sinuous snakes of plastic tubing that fed liquid into him and extracted fluids from his body. She would have to keep the neurological observations up every two hours throughout the night, checking his response to command, his grip and the level of contraction of his pupils to light.

Now, where to put her new arrival? Bed number one, near her desk, seemed a good idea.

'Nurse Peters, could you turn down that bed ready for a new patient on his way up from Casualty?' A great clatter at the doors proclaimed the arrival of two hospital porters pushing the patient in a regulation wheelchair.

'Where do you want him, Staff?' one of them called down the ward.

Dido walked briskly up to the small group. 'Hello, Mr Manetti. I'm Staff Nurse Alexander. Nurse Peters will help you to unpack and put on your pyjamas and Dr Brady will be in to see you in a while.' Then, turning her gaze to the porters she pointed to bed one. 'That bed over there, please.' They helped the small, middle-aged man out of the bulky wheelchair and into the chair by his bed.

Dido called the switchboard and asked them to bleep Russell Brady and then walked back to draw the faded curtains around Mr Manetti's bed. When the patient was comfortably ensconced, with his few belongings in the locker beside him, Nurse Peters joined Dido for the drugs round. Dido had already unlocked the drugs trolley and together they wheeled it over to the first bed on the right.

'How's the headache, Mr Stiller?' Dido walked over to the side of his bed and looked down on the young man lying with his eyes shut.

'A bit better, thanks,' he muttered, his brows knitting, either with pain or irritation. Then he opened his eyes and smiled briefly on recognising Dido. 'Oh, you're back, Staff. I've been cussing you all day for persuading me to stay for tests. That one this morning was terrible!' Dido took his hand, as much to check his pulse as to reassure him with a bit of human contact.

'I know, but we hope it'll get to the root cause of your symptoms and then perhaps we can start treating them for you. I've got some more pain-killers for you.' Dido handed them to him with a glass of water. 'These might make you constipated. If you have any trouble tell Nurse Peters. She's the bowel expert, she can make anyone go!' Despite himself, Mr Stiller laughed.

There was a sudden commotion at the doorway and Dido looked up to see Russell Brady practically fall into the ward, having caught his stethoscope on the door handle.

'God! I'm exhausted, Di—sorry, Staff Nurse,' he said apologetically as he realised Dido was in the middle of dealing with a patient. 'I'll get on and see Mr Manetti. Which bed?'

Dido pointed to where the curtains were still drawn. She continued on her round. Just as she was approaching the last patient, another new admission and a very sick one at that, Russell Brady emerged from his examination of Mr Manetti.

'I don't think he's too serious. Just keep an eye on him tonight, look out for disturbed behaviour. And warn the day staff to discreetly vet the gifts that come in to him at visiting time. We don't want any alcohol smuggled in in bunches of flowers, or laced orange juice, brought by well-meaning relatives. We should be able to do the biopsy tomorrow and will set his treatment on the results of that.'

As he spoke, his eye was caught by the pale, thin features of the young man in the last bed. Dido had not had time to read the notes on him, but knew Russell would be only too happy to fill her in on all the details.

'Ah, this one's a tricky case. Came in this morning. Infection of the heart valves. Bacterial endocarditis,' he announced importantly, as if he alone had been responsible for the diagnosis. Dido looked down at the notes.

'John Milsom. He's only twenty-four. How did he get the infection?'

'He went to the dentist without antibiotic protection. He'd had rheumatic fever as a child, which left him with a heart murmur. Dr Dauntcey saw him and ordered an echo-cardiograph. I'm afraid there's little doubt about the diagnosis.' Dido walked over to the side of the bed.

'Hello, John, I'm Staff Nurse Alexander and this is Dr Brady.' The patient smiled weakly up at her and she could see his face glistening with sweat. Picking up the towel from his chair she mopped his brow. 'It's important to keep up your fluid intake. When did you last have a drink?'

'About half an hour ago, a whole glass of water.'

'Good. Now, if anything worries you, if you find

yourself getting breathless or more feverish, you must ring this bell here.'

Dido and Dr Brady moved away from the bed, he taking her arm in an over-familiar way.

'It was great at the party last night. You looked fantastic. Who would have thought our prim, conscientious little staff nurse could be such a siren on the dance floor!'

'Oh, shut up, Russell, please.' Dido was embarrassed and irritated by his attentions. She was worried about Mr Milsom. She would have to be watching him carefully tonight and a lot of responsibility for him would fall on her shoulders. It was a dangerous game they had to play, withholding antibiotics until they had grown blood cultures and determined exactly what infection they had to treat. Her vigilance would be crucial . . .

'You'll be on call tonight in case anyone deteriorates?'

'Yes, sweetie, for you I'm on call any time. But, please God, let me off tonight and I'll promise to be good. I need my beauty sleep, just this once.' And he rolled his eyes beseechingly towards the ceiling.

'Well, if you didn't lead such a debauched social life there would be no need of divine intervention,' Dido said sweetly over her shoulder as she walked back to her desk and slipped Mr Milsom's notes into the trolley.

'My reputation does me a disservice. I'm really a lamb in wolf's clothing. Under all this,' and he plucked at his jacket and shirt, 'lurks the sweetest, gentlest soul.' His voice was light and jocular but Dido felt there was a part of him which was a hurt little boy, for all his confident extroversion and Lothario ways. She shooed him out of the ward, telling him that *she* at least had work to do.

It was already past ten o'clock and Dido and Nurse Peters went from bed to bed, switching off the lights, talking briefly to the patients and saying good night. At last the ward was quiet and dark, the only light emanating from the table lamp on her desk where she and Nurse Peters sat to write up the Kardex.

'We'll have to be particularly careful of Mr Milsom,' Dido said as she wrote down instructions for four-hourly readings of his temperature, blood pressure and pulse. 'Mr Stiller might have difficulty sleeping.' She looked up to where his body lay, a dark lump in the shadows.

The two women took it in turns to walk quietly from bed to bed, checking that all seemed well, that everyone had managed to get to sleep, and that their breathing was regular. She believed it was reassuring to the patients too, who, sometimes sleeping fitfully, were aware of the quiet presence of a nurse, the cool touch of her hand. It was on these routine rounds that pulse rate, blood pressure and other prescribed observations were made on the very sick patients.

It was nearly twelve o'clock. Nurse Peters had gone to the ward kitchen to make some coffee. Dido was checking Mr Milsom's pulse, counting it off against her watch, when she became aware of someone standing behind her. Still holding Mr Milsom's wrist, she turned in surprise and just managed to suppress a gasp as she found herself looking straight into the eyes of Dr Dauntcey.

'Sorry to startle you, Staff, but I've just come out of a meeting and thought I'd drop in to check on John Milsom here.'

His voice was quiet as he moved closer to the bedside to see the patient better. Dido's heart was hammering so hard she felt it must be audible, especially as the patient, observed so closely by Dr Dauntcey, seemed, in contrast, so motionless and quiet.

'How's he doing?' he asked without looking up.

'He seems to be holding his own,' Dido said evenly.

As James Dauntcey continued to observe the patient, checking his pulse again, he said in a voice so quiet it was almost a whisper, 'Before penicillin this had a one hundred per cent mortality rate. It was a terrible disease.'

Gently he woke the sleeping man and explained that he needed to look into his eyes with an ophthalmascope. While the doctor was deep in concentration Dido took the opportunity to look, really for the first time, at the man who had given her so much cause for regret and alarm these last few days. His straight, steely profile she knew already, but she had not noticed before how dark his hair was, almost black, and close-growing to the nape of his neck, curling slightly over the immaculate white collar of his shirt. But belying the stern contours of his face his lips were broad and infinitely kissable . . .

Dido pulled herself up short. How could she day-dream like that? This was the high and mighty consultant with whom she had already had a couple of unfortunate brushes. She was just a silly, feather-brained nurse in his opinion, if indeed she even merited an opinion at all.

'I'd just like to listen to his heart. See if that murmur's any worse.' Dr Dauntcey looked at Dido as he straightened up. He seemed very tall now, standing across the bed from her, and Dido lowered her eyes quickly and began to undo the buttons of Mr Milsom's pyjama top.

'Thanks, Staff.' Dr Dauntcey put his stethoscope round his neck and warmed the diaphragm with his hands before placing it precisely on the patient's chest. What lovely hands he had. Dido always noticed doctors' hands for they were so much in evidence in the daily routine of medicine. These hands holding the stethoscope were lean and brown with the shadow of dark hair curling from beneath his shirt cuff.

'Thank you.' Dr Dauntcey had finished his examination but as he moved away from the bed he seemed preoccupied and deep in thought.

Mr Milsom had already fallen asleep again and Dido gently fastened his pyjama jacket, pulled up the sheet and blankets, tucked him in and turned off the bed light. As she walked back to her desk she was surprised to see the doctor still on the ward, standing by her chair and looking into space.

'Would you like a coffee, sir?' Dido was feeling in need of one herself.

'What? Oh yes, I could do with one. Thanks, Staff.' Dido asked Nurse Peters to hold the fort for ten minutes as she led the way to Sister's office. There was just enough real coffee left from an earlier brewing and she turned on the machine to heat it up.

'I hope our conservative treatment of that young man will be proved right,' Dr Dauntcey said as he sat down with a sigh, a frown knitting his dark brows. 'Keeping a close watch on him is vital, Staff. You're doing an excellent job, I know. But what I'm afraid of is incipient heart failure. The moment there's any increased breathlessness, fall in blood pressure or rise in pulse, you must get Frank or even me in here on the double. If things get worse before we've got the results of the cultures we'll have no choice but to treat him with a cocktail of antibiotics and diuretics. But I hope with your nursing skills and my judgement that it won't get to that.'

He passed a weary hand over his face and then for the first time smiled. As he looked at Dido his pupils enlarged, his eyes appeared to darken and she, meeting his gaze, knew he was looking at her closely for the first time.

'Your hair is full of tiny diamonds, or is that a natural phenomenon, the sign of an angel?' He put out a hand to pick one of the sparkling fragments from her hair. Much to her chagrin, Dido felt a blush rise to her cheeks.

'It's only some glitter left from last night's party. I thought I'd brushed it all out.' And then, still uncomfortably aware of his amused gaze and for want of something to distract his attention, she said hesitantly, 'Have you enjoyed your first few days at St Benedict's?'

He relaxed and leant back in his chair. 'It's been so hectic I haven't had much time for enjoyment, but it's an excellent hospital. I like the team I work with too—and the nurses are particularly intelligent and perspicacious.' He cast her a fleeting sidelong glance that seemed to sparkle with humour. 'Particularly one red-headed staff nurse who seems to combine impeccable professional ability with a fiery temperament, both on and off duty.'

Dido thought immediately that he was referring to the party and said quickly, her fine skin blushing again, 'Oh, but I very seldom go out. Most of my energy goes into my work.'

James Dauntcey was suddenly serious and, looking down at his mug of coffee, he said, half to himself, 'It's important to go out and enjoy yourself. That's the trouble with medicine as a career, it too easily becomes all-absorbing.'

'But in your position don't you get more time off, a better chance of a private life?'

'Yes, I do. Theoretically I have much more regular time off than a houseman like Brady, or even senior registrars like Frank. But I have more responsibility. The buck stops with me. And so, for instance, with Mr

Milsom the ultimate decision about how we treat him is mine. That can take a lot of thought and energy. Perhaps I am too responsible.' Then his voice changed, becoming softer and more reflective, almost as if he were talking to himself. 'Certainly a woman I was very fond of told me she couldn't bear playing second fiddle to my career.' He looked up, still in that unguarded state, and Dido saw in that moment of vulnerability how hurt and isolated a part of him was.

Then, realising she was watching him, Dr Dauntcey snapped back unexpectedly into the cool professional. 'I suppose doctors like me are just married to our jobs and can't expect a woman to put up with that.'

Dido filled up his mug with the remains of the coffee. She wondered if he had made an unhappy marriage, or whether he still pined for the woman who had left. There was certainly a darkness, a desolation in the heart of the man, masked so effectively by those brooding good looks and professional confidence. He was looking at her again, the pain gone and his eyes full of that quizzical good humour.

'But what about you, Staff Nurse Alexander? You're much too clever and beautiful to ever be married to your job.'

'I don't think I'll be married to anyone or anything for a long time, if ever,' she said lightly, tossing off his question. 'I don't think doctor-nurse romances work very well, and I only seem to meet doctors. But I'm in no hurry.' She took his empty mug, relieved to have something to do to distract him from this line of questioning.

'I must be getting some sleep.' Dr Dauntcey stood up and turned to face her. 'About Mr Milsom—I'll order a daily portable chest X-ray so we can check any change in the size of the heart. The culture tests should be back in a few days—tomorrow if he's teeming with bugs—and then we can really start treating him. Keep up the good work, Staff. Don't hesitate to get me or Frank out of bed if there's any ominous change.' And, back in the persona of imperious consultant, he strode out of the door.

Dido walked slowly back to the ward. Her mind was full of speculation about his life and character and her heart touched by the glimpse of unexpected vulnerability.

CHAPTER FOUR

DIDO was woken from her welcome sleep by Millie putting a cup of tea on the table by her bed. She stretched and rolled over, feeling for her watch among the books and jars of face cream.

'Goodness, I've slept for ages! It's five already.' She sat up and swung her legs over the side of the bed, brushing her long hair back from her face. 'How was your day, Millie?' she called to her friend, who had walked through to the kitchen to make herself some toast.

'Oh, so-so. Nothing too dramatic, luckily. Although talking about dramatic . . .' She came back into Dido's bedroom in order to relate more effectively the story she had been waiting all day to tell. 'Your Dr Dauntcey seems to have a talent for the dramatic.'

'He's not *my* Dr Dauntcey!' Dido interjected, a little too hastily.

Millie continued unperturbed. 'At lunch today the canteen was abuzz.' She sat on the edge of the bed and looked curiously at Dido who was trying, unsuccessfully, to hide her intense curiosity.

'Oh, what about?' she asked coolly.

'Well,' Millie took a deep breath, 'James Dauntcey, or should I say Sir James, was lying in bed in his smart Belgravia mansion, listening to the early morning rattle and bang of the men erecting scaffolding outside . . .'

Dido laughed at the preamble. 'Come on Millie!' she remonstrated.

58

'When suddenly the illustrious doctor hears a cry and then a thump, just below his window. Grabbing a towel or bathrobe to cover his virile nakedness—'

Dido snorted derisively, 'Now I know you're prevaricating!'

'I shall continue,' Millie said haughtily. 'Covering his virile nakedness with a handy garment, our hero ran downstairs and onto the pavement. There he beheld a seriously injured scaffolder, lying prone on the ground. The young man was surrounded by his mates and as Dr Dauntcey pushed them aside and knelt by his head he noticed the young man had stopped breathing. Immediately he set to with mouth to mouth resuscitation and breathed life back into the boy.' Millie sighed and leaned back, obviously pleased with her own performance.

Dido was intrigued, even a little thrilled, by the story, but she was still sceptical. 'How do you know all this? I doubt Dr Dauntcey told you.'

'Ah, it's all absolutely true. Pat Townsend, an old room-mate of mine from student days, works on Neuro and she had to take down the sequence of events when they admitted the patient. By that time he was conscious and surprisingly lively and he filled in all the colourful details himself.'

'And you embellished them!' Dido laughed.

'Oh, not much. It's a good enough story on its own.'

'Well, fancy Dr Dauntcey living in Belgravia. St Ben's consultants usually plump for leafy Hampstead,' Dido mused.

'That's just what nosey old Pat said, and apparently this scaffolder told her it was the Dauntcey family's London home. Been in the family for a century or more.'

'Your talkative scaffolder seems a mine of information. The damage in the fall can't have been that critical,' Dido said as she finished her tea and started to get dressed.

'He's got a depressed fracture of the skull, serious enough to make him stop breathing.'

'Have they operated yet?' Dido looked up from buttoning the crisp cotton of her uniform.

'The moment they got him in. Looks good. There shouldn't be any permanent damage.'

Dido walked over to the window and looked out. 'It's raining again!' she complained. 'It must have started since you came in, Millie,' and she turned to her friend with a grimace. 'It's bound to be still bucketing down when I have to walk to the hospital. Just my luck!'

'Has your body-clock adjusted to night duty yet, Di?' Millie had bustled back into the kitchen and was making supper.

'Almost. I found it hard to get to sleep last night, but then I had rather a lot on my mind . . .' Dido's voice trailed off as she remembered her conversation with Dr Dauntcey, full of puzzles and conundrums about his own personal life which had set her speculating and wondering, spending far too much emotional energy on a man who hardly even noticed her.

'I really feel in need of a holiday but I'm not due any until the spring. I think a nice two weeks in Greece would suit me fine, just about Easter time when the wild flowers are spectacular,' Dido said airily, wondering how she was going to save enough money for that, especially with Christmas in between.

She ate supper quickly, a tasty fish pie Millie had put together in ten minutes, then washed up and briskly gathered her belongings together. Dido wanted to be early on the ward tonight, she hated being pressed for time. She checked quickly on the weather, still pouring with rain, and decided to don her green wellington boots and carry her shoes in her bag. Slipping into her rain-cape and pulling the hood over her golden head, Dido called goodbye to her friend and ran down the stairs into the street.

The rain hit her as if a bucket of water had been thrown in her face. It was too windy to put up her old umbrella so she bent her head, pulled the hood more closely round her face and started to walk rapidly towards the main road.

The heavy traffic streamed past her. It always seemed to double in volume the moment the first raindrop fell. Dido had to cross the road in order to avoid some pavement works and waited impatiently in the rain for a convenient gap in the double column of cars. Stepping further into the yellow glow of the street lamp, so that some charitable driver might notice her and slow to let her cross, Dido was enraged to find a great sheet of water surge up suddenly and drench her as a car pulled into the kerb at speed.

'Damned inconsiderate brute!' she muttered to her-self as she shook the front of her cape and wriggled her toes in her cold wet boots. She glared over towards the rear of the black limousine and was amazed to see a familiar dark head emerge, shielded from the downpour by an enormous gold-tipped black umbrella.

'Want a lift, Staff?' Dr Dauntcey was smiling as he held the umbrella over her head.

'Oh, thank you, I will,' Dido said rather stiffly. Then, looking down at her cape running with water, she hesitated. 'I'd better not. I'm so wet I might waterlog your car.'

'Don't be silly, Staff. My car's put up with worse things than a bit of honest rain. Climb in,' he ordered— rather too peremptorily for Dido's liking, but it would have been ungracious to argue. The idea of a nice warm, dry five-minute ride to hospital was tempting indeed.

'It's lucky you were standing under that light, otherwise I wouldn't have recognised you, bundled up in that mac.' Dr Dauntcey gave her a sidelong smile which was both slightly mocking and yet familiar and provocative. Sitting in such close proximity in the warm, dimly-lit interior of his Rolls-Royce, Dido suddenly felt shy and a little self-conscious. She knew she probably looked a fright with a bright red nose, rain on her face and the unbecoming hood pulled low over her brow. She casually pushed the hood from her hair, releasing a cascade of raindrops in the process. The fronds of hair that framed her face had grown more unruly in the wet and they curled in red-gold profusion around her fine flushed skin.

The silence seemed to make his presence all the more intimate and unsettling. Dido felt she had to speak. 'It's very kind of you to offer me a lift. I would've looked like a drowned rat by the time I got to St Ben's.'

'Not a drowned rat, I think—with your colouring, more like a little drowned fox. A little golden vixen!' and he laughed. It was the first time Dido had seen James Dauntcey really amused and she watched, fascinated, as he threw back his head, uttering a rich throaty laugh, his blue eyes crinkled and dancing, so transformed from the cool, challenging gaze of his professional mien.

Then, as the meaning of his last words sank into her consciousness, she wondered how pointed he had meant to be. A vixen indeed!

'I don't know that I like that analogy,' she said coolly,

purposefully turning her head away and watching the raindrops course down the window.

'Exactly. I wouldn't expect less of you. You're strong-minded, perverse and opinionated and you disagree with most of what I say. You'd make some poor devil an excellent wife.' And he laughed again, but this time it was a quiet chuckle, almost as if he was enjoying a private joke.

'I don't intend to make anyone an excellent wife!' Dido snapped, her colour rising.

'Heading for the post of Matron instead, then?' James Dauntcey cast her a quizzical glance and for a moment Dido was quite taken aback by how handsome he looked, his eyes gleaming in the reflected light of the passing cars and his features made even more dramatic by the play of brilliant light and inky shadow. His hands on the wheel drove the big car with consummate ease. Dido was only aware of whether they were in motion or stationary by the registering of the speedometer.

'Perhaps,' Dido evaded his question. 'I haven't thought much beyond being a sister, I enjoy working on the wards so much.'

He smiled and his next question took her by surprise. 'Did you ever think of training to be a doctor?'

'No. Not when I left school. I was just so keen to get onto the wards and start nursing sick people.' Dido paused and looked away. 'But now, I suppose I regret sometimes not being able to make important decisions and always having to defer to doctors, some of whom, especially the students, know less than I do and don't have the grace to acknowledge it.'

'I hope you don't think all doctors are as arrogant as that.'

Dido looked quickly across at Dr Dauntcey, but she

could learn very little from his steely, immobile profile. 'No, of course not! Your confidence is totally justified.' Her voice trailed off as she realised just how her hasty words could have been taken the wrong way.

But Dr Dauntcey had not misunderstood her and in the same quiet, inscrutable voice he said, 'Similarly, not all nurses are as intelligent and perceptive as you.' He had just turned the long, gleaming black bonnet of his car in through the gateway of St Benedict's. 'Only the other night, for instance, one of the nurses here was mooning along in the middle of the road and nearly got herself run down. I mean, if someone like that can't even look after herself, how can we entrust her with important decisions about her patients?'

Dido managed to stifle the gasp of anger and dismay that rose in her throat as she realised just who that nurse had been. How dare he blame her for his own recklessly fast driving? But she could not reveal to him that she was that nurse. Why, she wondered, did she need this man's approval? Was it more than a desire for his professional admiration? As Dr Dauntcey opened the passenger door for her, Dido was shaken to realise just how much his good opinion mattered to her.

She ducked her head against the rain and thanked him hurriedly for the lift, running through the dark towards the lighted entrance. As she pushed her way through the glass doors she saw reflected in them the dark figure of Dr Dauntcey, standing by the still-open passenger door, his head unprotected from the rain, gazing after her. That image of him, silent and still, his thoughts unfathomable, remained with her as she walked briskly up to Millington ward.

Staff Nurse Julie Williams was taking the pulse of Mr Jameson when Dido arrived. She had hung up her dripping cape and changed into her ward shoes and felt almost dry again.

'Hello, Julie.' She walked quietly up to her side. Together they looked down on poor Mr Jameson, the patient with the sub-arachnoid haemorrhage. 'He doesn't look any better. I suppose there's been no improvement in his responses?' Dido spoke quietly, for although Mr Jameson was in a coma she believed that one should never speak about such patients as if they could not hear or feel or respond.

'No, unchanged. We've managed to clear up that infection though. But the two-hourly turning is important and quite difficult to fit in when the ward is hectic.'

They had moved away from his bed and Julie Williams turned to the desk to consult her notes and give Dido any new information on the patients before going off duty. 'We're still treating his blood pressure with Hydralazine. It seems to be doing the trick. Oh, and of course, clearing his airway with the ward suction pump. That trusty machine has been quite busy, as you'll see with our new admission!' She looked towards the bed by the ward doors where an old man appeared to be asleep.

'Mr Manton, Sam, as apparently he likes to be called, is a dosser from the men's hostel down the road. He's diabetic. Russell Brady says he's quite a regular visitor, neglects to inject his insulin and ends up here.'

'So he's in coma and I suppose hyperventilating, dehydrated?' Dido walked over to look at the old chap.

She could smell the acetone on his breath, a sure sign of diabetic keto-acidosis. She turned to Julie Williams and whispered, 'How old is he? Much younger than he looks, I'll be bound.'

'Well, the warden who brought him in said he's forty-two, but it's hard to believe.'

Dido looked down at his mass of grey hair, none too clean—but then his personal hygiene was the least of their worries at this stage. His face in repose was wrinkled and benign, rather like a snoozing Father Christmas. The fever had flushed his cheeks a festive pink and Dido looked forward to nursing him back to health, getting him to bath and feeding him up on hospital food, which to these homeless, nomadic men was equivalent to feasting at the Ritz.

She looked at the drip. 'Who's treating him?' she asked Julie.

'Oh, Russell is. He hasn't involved Frank. He ordered a half-normal saline drip and he's taking arterial blood samples from his femoral artery every hour. We pack these in a beaker filled with ice and send them to the lab to measure blood gases and acid-base.'

'Of course, he's also on insulin by continuous infusion from that pump,' Dido said, listening again to the patient's rasping breathing and deciding she would be much happier if he was turned further onto his side. 'Here, help me Julie. I think he should be propped further over. I don't like the sound of his chest.'

Together, they tilted him over, bending his knee to balance him better and taking care not to pull the drip needle from his arm.

'I suppose Dr Brady left instructions to aspirate him hourly. Oh, and where's the chest X-ray?'

'Well, there isn't one. Dr Brady seemed to think it unnecessary as Sam's been in so many times before. He's treating him as he's done before. For straight diabetic coma.'

They walked back to the desk and Julie Williams continued with her briefing.

'Mr Manetti, suspected alcoholic cirrhosis. We'll be able to do his liver biopsy tomorrow. His blood liver function tests have come back from the lab and they show the liver damage is quite severe. We've also had our work cut out for us at visiting time,' Julie broke off with a laugh. Mr Manetti's jolly face turned in her direction and she dropped her voice.

'He has had a stream of the most colourful friends and relatives trooping in here. I'm sure half the East End Mafia have passed through our ward doors. My nurses were discreetly taking their presents before they got into the patient's hands.'

Dido's eyes were dancing. 'What did they find?'

'A lovely bunch of chrysanthemums cleverly disguised a half-bottle of Scotch and the cake his mum brought in was so alcoholic it's a miracle it didn't burst into flames in her hands.' The two women chuckled together and Dido regretted not being on days so that she could meet this colourful crew.

'He looks quite cheery. Is the Heminevrin keeping the worst of his withdrawal symptoms at bay? Or do you think he's found a supply of liquor you've all overlooked?' Dido giggled again.

'No. I'm sure he's dry. He's just an ebullient, tough character. Takes things as they come.'

'How's our MS suspect, Mr Stiller? He's neither ebullient nor tough.' Dido looked over to the young man who was propped up in bed reading a motoring magazine.

'The National Hospital for Nervous Diseases at Queen Square has got some of his spinal fluid and we should get those results quite soon. He went today to the neurology department here for his VER tests, you know, where they show him a changing checker-board pattern and then measure his responses by means of electrodes placed at the back of the head.'

'How did he do?' Dido was intrigued. She knew that these visually evoked response tests were very effective at indicating the presence of multiple sclerosis. An abnormal response meant MS was a likely diagnosis.

'The neurology chaps haven't given their formal verdict yet, but there's no doubt that there's something not quite right.'

'It's what I feared.' Dido looked again at the young man with real compassion in her eyes. The worst aspect of the disease was not so much that it could not be cured but its unpredictable nature, its cruel attack and retreat, the impossibility of giving a sufferer any definite prognosis. She turned to Julie. 'It's odd that although women are more prone to the disease, I think one and a half times more get it than men, men tend to be more severely affected.'

'I know. My cousin, a woman, has had it for fifteen years and luckily it seems to be quite a benign form. At least she's still mobile.'

'Is Mr Stiller's headache better?'

'Yes. That codeine phosphate kept it under control and now he only needs the occasional dose. His spirits are quite good too.'

'So he's not threatened to discharge himself again?' Dido smiled, remembering how calming him down had earned her the disapprobation of their new consultant.

'No. He seems to be resigned to finding out the truth about his condition.'

'Mr Milsom, with the endocarditis, is still very sick but he seems to be holding his own.' Dido followed Julie's eyes to where John Milsom lay flat in his bed, a drip up ready to take the large doses of antibiotics when the bug responsible for his infected heart valve was identified.

She remembered James Dauntcey's concern about him last night and asked Julie Williams, 'Is Dr Dauntcey satisfied with his progress?'

'He's been in a couple of times to look at him. I think he feels his conservative approach is paying off. We're just on tenterhooks, hoping the results from the bug cultures come through soon.'

'I suppose today's chest X-ray showed no enlargement of the heart, otherwise Dr Dauntcey would have had to fill him up with a cocktail of antibiotics and diuretics, just hoping to hit on the right one.'

Julie shook her head. 'No, nothing's changed from yesterday, so here's hoping he stays that way,' and she crossed her fingers as she walked off to Sister's office to collect her cape and umbrella. 'See you tomorrow,' she waved and left.

Dido consulted the Kardex. Sam Manton was due to be aspirated. She collected a pair of disposable gloves, the ward suction pump and a new rubber catheter to fit on the nozzle. Russell Brady would be in soon to take the arterial blood sample.

Diabetic coma was an unpopular condition to treat. It meant the poor houseman could not go to bed for he, not the nurses, had to take the blood samples and adjust the treatment accordingly. This was one of the rules which irritated Dido, for she knew she would be just as efficient as most doctors and more efficient than Russell. But medical traditions were the last to change and Dido had long ago given up kicking against the system.

She wheeled the pump over to Mr Manton's bedside and plugged it into the socket in the wall. Dido then put on the pair of gloves and picked up the rubber tube of the suction pump. His breathing was very rattley and it concerned her. She would have been much happier if Dr Brady had ordered a chest X-ray; she was always afraid that these homeless men who so neglected themselves, rarely saw a doctor from one year to the next, might have tuberculosis. It was a disease so easily masked by bronchitis, smoker's chest and all the other ailments these poor men were subject to.

She leaned over Mr Manton and gently opened his mouth, noticing the surprisingly good state of his teeth. So many she had nursed had appalling mouthfuls of rotting teeth, but Sam's were strong, certainly discoloured, but all there, his haliotosis partially masked by the sweet scent of acetone on his breath. She turned on the pump and squeezed the soft rubber tubing between her fingers as, with the other hand, she directed it at the back of his throat. Then, alternately releasing and squeezing the catheter, she cleared his throat of the accumulated sputum.

Sam Manton still seemed to be in deep coma. Given that they had been treating him with a continuous slow infusion of insulin for seven hours now, she would have expected some sign of consciousness.

There was the familiar bang of the ward doors and Dido glanced up to see Russell Brady enter, looking rather the worse for wear.

'You're a welcome sight, Di,' he said as he walked over to her desk. 'I'm so tired I can hardly see straight. I've come to take Sam Manton's blood. Can you help me get him onto his back so I can find his femoral artery?'

Dido placed a restraining hand on Russell's arm. She wanted to speak to him before he bustled back within earshot of Mr Manton. 'I'm concerned about that patient. Shouldn't he be coming round by now?'

Russell answered tiredly, 'He's been in before. He's a regular and each time it's because he's neglected to shoot his insulin. He took quite a while to respond last time, if I remember correctly.'

But Dido still was not happy. 'What about his chest? It sounds pretty bad to me.'

'Oh, you clever nurses! You think you're dab hands at diagnosis! I know what you're driving at,' and Russell Brady put his hands on his hips and laughed condescendingly. 'No, he hasn't got TB. He's just a heavy smoker. These old lags have all sorts of complaints, but his main problem is diabetes and that's what I'm treating. OK, Staff?' Dido felt her cheeks flush with anger at Dr Brady's put-down.

She followed him to Sam Manton's bed and wordlessly helped Russell to roll him gently onto his back. The rattle in his breathing increased and she looked sharply at Russell, but he was busy preparing his syringe, plunging the needle first into the anti-coagulant Heparin and then swabbing Mr Manton's groin before probing gently for the main artery.

Dido watched the bright blood spurt into the glass syringe, pushing the plunger up to the required mark. She pressed on the puncture site with her thumb for the regulation two minutes, checked that the patient was not bleeding and stuck a small square of plaster on the spot. They rolled him back onto his side. Throughout the whole procedure he did not stir, and his uneven, rasping breath continued to worry Dido.

Dr Brady handed her the phial of blood and collected together his notes.

'Bye, Di. Stop worrying. See you in an hour's time.'

And he left to return to his cell-like room to try and grab a cat-nap.

Dido had a ward full of other sick patients who needed attention too. She motioned to Nurse Peters, on duty again with her that evening. 'Anne, let's divide up the ward. You do the right-hand side and I'll do the left.' Then, looking closely at the young nurse, Dido noticed she was pinched and pale. 'Are you all right?' she asked her solicitously.

Anne Peters nodded and looked down quickly at the Kardex, making a show of checking on the treatment details of the patients she would be seeing. Dido knew from the nurses' grapevine that Nurse Peters was madly in love with a student doctor, one Jake Gillespie, a handsome, assured young man who would go far and fast up the medical hierarchy. Dido's heart went out to the young nurse who was obviously having to cope with her first broken heart.

'Do you want to talk about it?' she asked gently as she gathered together the papers on her desk.

'There's nothing to say,' Anne said miserably.

'Is it all over?' Dido's voice was quiet and sympathetic.

'Yes,' Anne said flatly. Then, turning to look at Dido, her eyes bright with tears, she added in a rush, 'I know it's ridiculous but I feel so desperately sad and empty, as if life's not worth living. And I'm only twenty-two!' She managed a small ironic laugh.

'I know,' Dido touched her arm, 'and if it's any consolation to you I've been there too; I've felt the same way and I've survived to live another day and love again.'

Dido was taken by surprise by her own words. Only a few weeks before she had been thinking, too, that she was proof against falling in love again. Yet here she was, consoling another young woman with words of hope that seemed to come from a deeper part of herself than her waking conscious mind. She smiled one of her big warm smiles and part of her radiance came from the recognition of a fundamental change in her being.

Anne Peters smiled back. 'Oh, Di, you're a brick. It does help to know one's not unique, and that this emptiness will pass.'

'Right then, back to work!' And Dido took her arm and set her off up the right side of the ward, visiting each patient in turn.

Dido finished her share of monitoring and pulse taking and collected the trolley with the suction pump. Sam Manton would be ready for his next aspiration. She walked over to his bed and looked closely at him. His coma seemed as deep as ever, the rattle in his chest was as loud, louder even, with the added amplification of the sputum in his throat. She leaned over him, opened his mouth and went through the same procedure:

Nurse Peters was still busy with her half of the ward, so Dido decided to take the pump to the sluice and rinse it out herself. On opening it up, she was alarmed to see streaks of blood amongst the sputum she had just aspirated from Sam Manton's throat. Saving it to show to Russell Brady, she quickly stripped off her disposable gloves, washed her hands thoroughly and strode back into the ward to ring him.

In her haste and concern, she failed to notice the tall dark figure leaning over John Milsom's bed. She was quickly connected with Dr Brady's phone. A sleepy voice answered.

'Russell, I've just found blood in Mr Manton's sputum. Would you come and see him?'

Russell yawned. 'Oh, Staff Nurse, really! You've probably been a bit too vigorous in your aspirating. I'll have a look at him when I'm next due to take his blood. I've got half an hour more, now leave me in peace.'

He put the phone down and Dido stood staring at the receiver in her hand, a rage of frustration rising in her. It would be quite unethical for her to go over Brady's head to Frank Berenson, his senior registrar, but how else could she get this patient properly tested?

Her enraged thoughts were interrupted by a light gripping of her shoulder. In the darkened ward, her attention absorbed totally by the problem in hand, she was startled by this unexpected touch. Turning quickly, her heart was set beating all the faster as she met the eyes of Dr James Dauntcey gazing down at her, his dark features even darker in the dim ward light. Only his eyes reflected light and they were mesmerising in their gleaming intensity.

'I seem to be making a habit of haunting your ward at night. My apologies.' He bowed slightly but a small smile played on his lips, making the gesture less formal and more provocative. Dido did not speak and he continued, 'I was called in by my registrar to look at a patient on Hartland ward and I thought I'd check our endocarditis while I was here. I'm most relieved to see he's not deteriorating. I hope to be able to start treatment tomorrow.' Then he peered closer at Dido's face. 'You look worried, Staff. Is anything the matter?'

'I'm a little puzzled by our new admission, Mr Manton, over there.' Before she could continue, James Dauntcey's tall, dark-suited figure had strode over to Sam's bedside and was leaning over his comatose body.

'Diabetic coma.' His words were brusque. 'Who admitted him?'

'Dr Brady,' Dido replied, equally shortly.

'What's going into him then?' he said, looking at the rate of drip from the saline bottle into the tub connected to Sam's body.

'Half-normal saline with added potassium and a slow infusion of insulin.'

Dr Dauntcey nodded, his piercing gaze flicking from the patient back to Dido's face, his expression grave and unchanging. 'What's his blood pressure?'

'Low, ninety over fifty.'

'And pulse?'

'One hundred and thirty.' As Dido answered he leaned over the grey-haired man and lifted his eyelids to examine his pupils.

'How long has he been in coma?'

'About eight hours now.' Dido did not feel it was her place to voice her concern about the unusually long time.

'I don't like the sound of his chest. Where's his chest X-ray?' Dr Dauntcey's questions and commands when investigating a patient's case left very little room for the finer conversational skills and social niceties.

'He hasn't had one,' Dido said quietly, embarrassed at having to show up Russell Brady in front of his boss.

'What do you mean?' Dr Dauntcey snapped at her, straightening up to his full height, a deep frown clouding his brow.

'Dr Brady's treated this patient a few times before and thought it unnecessary . . .' Dido was interrupted by the icy voice of a very angry consultant.

'Get Brady up here immediately! And call the portable X-ray people. I want a sputum test, too.'

Dido knew she and Russell Brady were for the high jump but she saw little merit in pointing out her observations and fears about an incomplete diagnosis of Mr Manton's condition. It was Russell's place to take the blame on himself. She called him up, summoned the radiographers and walked back to the bedside where Dr Dauntcey stood, deep in thought and hatchet-faced.

'And could you ask your nurse to prepare the bed in that side ward in case isolation is called for?' he rapped out.

'Yessir!' Dido could not help a slightly mocking inflection from creeping into her voice. She understood his concern—she felt it too—but saw no reason for such imperious behaviour.

There was a flurry of movement and then the clatter of the ward doors as Russell burst in, crumple-faced and tousled. He cast Dido a sheepish glance and then walked quickly over to his chief.

'After we've seen the X-ray results I may need a lumbar puncture. Staff has sent off a sample of sputum to the lab to be stained for tubercle bacilli. The radiographers are due any minute.' Dr Dauntcey was cold and precise. There was no word of accusation or condemnation. Not yet.

The ward doors clattered again and Dido, seeing the sleepy radiographers arriving on the ward behind their portable X-ray machine, moved over quickly to Mr Manton's bedside. They needed her help in lifting him to sitting position to slip the plate behind his back. Dr Dauntcey watched it all impassively and then turned on his heel to return to his critical patient on Hartland ward.

Dido had glanced at him once, briefly, and had seen a

vein throbbing on his right temple. She could not imagine what black thoughts coursed beneath that expressionless mask. But the passion in the man, whether in anger, as Dido had experienced it, or in love, was a palpable force only just contained by his steely self-control. Dido had felt this force as she stood beside him, an electric presence that made the nape of her neck tingle, made her more sensitive to sound, to smell, to touch, made her more aware of everything, particularly the tall, dark man beside her. Now he had gone there seemed a vacuum where he had once stood. Into that emptiness Russell's voice intruded.

'He won't need a lumbar puncture. I'm going off for a coffee.' Dido turned to see him walk through into Sister's office to pour himself a cup.

The radiographers had really worked fast, for within half an hour the phone rang—the film was on its way. Dido replaced the telephone receiver and looked up to see the stern figure of James Dauntcey return to her ward. He walked right up to her, standing so close that she could feel his breath on her cheek, could smell the warm maleness of him. Dido felt she ought to take a step backwards, but he seemed to be oblivious to her proximity. He neither looked at her nor spoke, his thoughts engrossed and distant.

Then suddenly Dr Brady's voice broke the uneasy silence. 'The film's arrived.' He held out a black negative.

Dr Dauntcey took it impatiently and walked over to the light box, slipped the film into the clips and switched on the bulb. He let his breath out with a soft whistle. It was clear for all to see. The lung fields were speckled with little lentil-sized deposits of infection.

'Miliary TB,' Dido said quietly, the first to speak.

Dr Dauntcey snapped off the light, his blue eyes inscrutable in a grim face.

He turned to Russell Brady. 'Right, Brady, get that lumbar puncture done and then we'll isolate him and start treatment.'

For the first time, Dido felt a sympathy for Russell. His tired brain had been shocked by the diagnosis and his evident negligence, and now it had to slip into top gear and remember the treatments for tuberculosis. It was worse than Finals. Russell dithered and Dr Dauntcey angrily repeated himself.

'I want to see if the poor devil's got tuberculous meningitis. So get on with the lumbar puncture.' He turned to Dido and without a glimmer of a smile said, 'I'll get some coffee. I presume there's some hot in Sister's office?' Dido nodded and turned to set up the trolley.

She disinfected the top of the trolley and placed on it a lumbar puncture pack, mask, gloves, local anaesthetic, some iodine skin preparation and a number of specimen containers. Dr Brady meanwhile prepared for the puncture procedure. He was tired and pale but unhesitatingly he stripped off his white coat, rolled his sleeves up and washed his hands. He returned to where Dido waited by the still comatose figure of Sam Manton.

'He's already on his left side,' she said quietly, handing him the gloves and mask. She watched Russell Brady perform a procedure she had seen a hundred times before, but each time there was a slight apprehension in her as he swabbed the lumbar region with iodine and then counted the vertebrae to check he had the right space, between the third and fourth lumbar vertebrae. In went the local anaesthetic, even though the poor patient was in coma, and then the glistening six-inch lumbar puncture needle was gently inserted between the relevant bumps on Sam Manton's spine.

It seemed smooth enough. Dido let out a small sigh of relief. She did not have the stamina for any more dramas on the ward tonight. Then Dr Brady removed the wire that ran up the inside of the needle and they watched as a few drops of cerebro-spinal fluid emerged. Dr Brady collected it in three different specimen bottles, but they could both see that it was slightly cloudy.

'O-oh, looks bad,' Russell said, turning even paler. Her phone rang again and Dido crossed swiftly to her desk.

'Millington ward, Mr Samuel Manton?' The lab technician's voice enquired.

'Yes, Staff Nurse Alexander here. Have you the results?' Dido asked quickly.

'Specimen heavily infected with acid-fast bacilli,' was the deadpan reply. Dido immediately called the porters—she would need help transferring the patient into isolation in the side ward. She put aside a mask and gloves for herself, the same for Nurse Peters and for Dr Brady. She took a set through to Sister's office where Dr James Dauntcey sat drinking coffee and reading his notes.

He looked up as she entered, the lamplight falling on his glossy dark hair and the high angle of his cheekbone. Dido noticed how dark his cheeks and chin were, shadowed with almost a whole day's growth of beard, and she realised that he had probably been up and working since early that morning. She glanced at the clock on the wall, it was nearly one. Her heart went out to him. He needed so much to be looked after, she thought, and then acknowledged with reluctance how much she would like to do the looking after.

Their eyes met for a moment, hers warm and amber-flecked, his intensely blue, an unfulfilled yearning in their depths, and for that instant Dido felt there was an emotional recognition, an intense need that flashed from him to her. Don't be foolish, her head admonished her heart, and abruptly James Dauntcey looked away.

'What is it, Staff?' His tone of voice denied any possible connection or vulnerability that in that previous moment she had believed to exist.

'Lab results on the sputum. Heavily infected with acid-fast bacilli,' she said in a businesslike way.

'Only to be expected.' Dr Dauntcey looked back at her. 'Call Dr Brady in here, please, Staff.'

Both Dido and Russell Brady knew that the time of reckoning had come. Dr Dauntcey was standing when they returned to Sister's office. His height, a great advantage in any circumstance, made him seem particularly powerful that night. He looked from one to the other as he spoke in cold, measured tones.

'Tonight has seen an example of medical negligence which I would not have expected of a cottage hospital, let alone one of the leading teaching hospitals in the world.' His unwavering gaze never left their faces as he continued. 'That patient should have had a chest X-ray the moment he was admitted. Given his poor social circumstances, a chest X-ray was routine. Then there were other clinical signs, the rattle, the blood-stained sputum, the prolonged coma and, for heaven's sake, you should have noticed the neck stiffness, a sure sign of meningitis.'

Dido felt her colour rise with anger and humiliation. Her heart sank sickeningly into the pit of her stomach. Dr Dauntcey was right, but it was so unfair of him to take it for granted that she had not done her job, observing the patient and reporting anything out of the ordinary. Once more she was branded by him as second-rate and inefficient. How could she ever have felt there was some communication, some sympathy between them? Why, there was not the first glimmering of an understanding . . .

And Russell! How cowardly of him not to stick up for her and put the record straight with his boss. He professed to love her and yet had not the guts and honesty to own up that she had noticed the patient's symptoms and had mentioned the possibility of TB.

It was sickeningly unfair and Dido's eyes flashed with indignation as she fought back the tears of frustration that threatened to spill down her cheeks. Her fine skin had flushed a fiery pink, which deepened as she caught James Dauntcey looking at her with such an unfathomable expression in his eyes she had to look away. She had to hide from his gaze her own turbulent emotions, so close to the surface now she feared he would read her like a book.

He had finished his catalogue of their short-comings and, turning on his heel, said as a parting shot, 'I am surprised and disappointed at such gross negligence and lack of basic intelligence. I hope this is the first and last time I have to say so.' Then, tapping Russell on the shoulder, he added, 'Brady, come with me. Try and vindicate yourself a little by helping me diagnose a puzzling case.'

That was too much for Dido. When the men had departed she sat down in Sister's chair and burst into tears of bitter anger and self-pity.

'How unfair! How unfair!' she muttered to herself, clenching her fists on the desk. How unfair to give Russell a chance to vindicate himself and leave her damned. There and then Dido vowed to give up the profession she had loved so much and marry the first man who asked her.

CHAPTER FIVE

AT LAST Dido's duty was over. She wearily collected her rain-cape, put on her wellingtons and collected her bag. She felt inordinately tired, in contrast to the new morning full of bird-song which greeted her. She emerged into the outside world blinking slightly, blown a little more awake by the fresh chill breeze which whisked round the quad. It was always slightly strange, leaving the cocoon-like world of the hospital, especially after night duty when the separateness of hospital life was particularly marked.

The walk back to the flat was a period of readjustment for Dido. At first she was shocked by the noise of the traffic, her nostrils assaulted by the acrid smell of exhaust on the air. She looked up at the patch of blue above to try and determine what the weather had in store that day. The wintry sky was blown clear of clouds by the night's storm and the sun was gleaming palely over rooftops. In hospital the temperature was constant, the lights eternal and artificial and the vagaries of climate seemed a whole world away.

As Dido left the hospital gates and with them her responsibility for her patients, the full weight of her despair settled dully on her shoulders. Not even the bustling streets, the friendly shopkeepers putting their wares out on display on the pavements, could lift her spirits. Perhaps she should give it all up and apply as a mature student for university? Dido pondered the pros and cons as she walked, buying a paper from the woman on the corner who was always so cheery, regardless of the weather or time of day.

She climbed the stairs to the flat slowly, hoping Millie would still be there. As she walked into the hall she was greeted by the delicious, welcoming aroma of freshly-brewed coffee and warm toast.

'Is that you, Di?' Millie's voice floated from the kitchen.

'Hello, Millie. I *am* glad you're still here,' Dido said, easing off her wellingtons and padding in bare feet through to the kitchen.

'Well, I'd better not offer you coffee if you're going to bed, but have some toast.'

'Yes, please,' Dido said, pulling up a stool and perching alongside her friend. 'We hardly see each other when we're on different duties like this. Are you OK?' She looked closely at Millie, noticing her ebullient friend looked uncharacteristically pale and a little drawn.

'I'm all right. We're just working very hard. Suddenly the City seems to be full of men having heart attacks. And some so young, too. You get a very biased view of life.' She smiled wanly, 'I sometimes find myself thinking you and I'll be lucky to survive past forty. But then I remember that we only see the ill fraction of the population. The hale and hearty don't come near us.' She smiled again and resumed her breakfast.

'Do you enjoy nursing, Millie?' Dido's speckled-gold eyes were still looking at her friend with a disconcerting intensity.

'That's a leading question to ask me so early in the morning! Of course I enjoy nursing. You'd have to, to put up with the hours, the strain—and the pay,' Millie added ruefully. Then looking sharply at Dido's unsmiling face she said, 'Why, don't you?'

Dido thought for a moment and then said, 'I just don't know if the advantages outweigh the disadvantages any more. I used to love nursing. It was my vocation. As you know, I'd always wanted to be a nurse and never wavered in my dedication, but just recently I've been feeling the hours make it so difficult to have much life outside the job. The job is so demanding and sometimes so unrewarding . . .'

'Hang on a moment,' Millie broke in, 'you sound as if you're trying to convince yourself of something. Unrewarding? I thought you felt it was the most rewarding thing in the world, caring for sick people and nursing them back to health. Why's that suddenly unrewarding?'

'Oh, that hasn't changed. The patients are as worthwhile and as responsive as ever. I suppose it's the doctors. Working for some of them is such a thankless task,' Dido finished rather lamely.

'Di! This isn't like you. Since when has the arrogance of a few pig-ignorant medical students got you down? You've always known how to cope with them.' Then as the truth dawned on Millie, she smiled. 'O-oh. It's not students, it's consultants isn't it? It's one particularly handsome one in particular? What's he been up to?' Millie crossed her arms over her chest as if she was housewife ready for a chinwag with a neighbour on her doorstep.

Dido had to smile. 'I know it's silly. Perhaps on night duty, when you're tired, everything gets a bit out of proportion. But it's awful being treated like an unobservant fool, when all along I had been thoroughly efficient and observant. Just prevented from action by a know-all houseman.'

'Oh yes. Russell Brady! Well, I hope he got what's been coming to him for months.'

'We *both* got it, and that's what's so galling. I was
tarred with the same brush and then Dr Dauntcey takes
him off to vindicate himself by helping diagnose another
patient!' Dido felt near to tears again.

'Come on, Di, you're just tired. It's particularly mad-
dening for someone like you who gives her all to the job.
But surely it's still worth all the effort?' Millie put her
arms round her friend's shoulders. 'You're the best
nurse I've ever come across. And Frank, for one, thinks
the same. You mustn't be so affected by the whims of
one consultant in a big hospital. Even if he is the best
looking one we've ever had!' And she squeezed Dido,
who gasped indignantly.

'But Millie, it's not that I fancy him, it's just that I like
to be seen to be doing a good job!'

Millie had walked to the sink to wash up and
she turned and said over her shoulder, 'Sure. It's
got absolutely nothing to do with him being attract-
ive!' She giggled and ducked as Dido threw her toast
crust.

Dido picked up her plate and washed it too. She felt so
much better. How extraordinary that just sharing one's
problems halved them, or in some cases dispersed them
all together.

'Thanks, Millie. I feel it's all much more in perspec-
tive. I'll sleep well now.'

'Well, I remember the times you've talked me out of
my blues.' Millie patted her on the back. 'It would be a
crime if you gave up nursing, you know.'

'Actually, I don't think I will.' With that, Dido padded
into her bedroom to get ready for bed.

Dido arrived at the hospital that night feeling fresh and
fighting fit. She had had a really good sleep and perhaps

she had adjusted at last to the routine of night duty. As she walked onto the ward her attention was immediately attracted by a new patient at the far side. He was an old, white-haired man who sat bolt upright in bed, his back as straight as a young man's. The light from his lamp illuminated his hair like a halo as he turned his head when she entered.

'Staff Nurse!' he called as she moved towards the desk. Dido walked over to him with a faint smile on her face. 'Hello, Staff Alexander,' the old man said in his rich, mellifluous voice. Dido's expression turned to one of polite enquiry. How did he know her name? What did he want?

'Don't you remember me?' His twinkly blue eyes crinkled up in a broad smile. 'Peregrine Salmon, Perry to you, you nursed me when you were a student, a wee slip of a girl. Now look at you. Staff Nurse! Very impressive.'

Dido stood by his bed, looking down on his handsome old face, and slowly she did remember. He had been a delight and she had grown very fond of him in the couple of weeks she had helped nurse him. She beamed her warmest smile.

'Yes, I do remember you. You're an artist—I even remember seeing an exhibition of your paintings a couple of years ago. But I can't remember what you were in for.'

The old man roared with laughter and then clutched at his chest, but continued to chuckle. 'You should have remembered, we laughed enough about it. I had piles!' And he chuckled again.

'Yes, I do!' and Dido laughed too and took his hand. 'But what are you in for now?'

'Ah, it's my old ticker. It's very tired. I think it's done

its bit for me, my dear.' His smile crinkled his wise old face.

'Well, I don't know that you can bow out quite that easily. With my expert nursing and your appetite for life we'll have you dancing again,' Dido said, and they both laughed at the memory of the day he was discharged last time, when he had grabbed her and waltzed her round the ward.

'Now I must go and relieve the day staff and get my briefing. Then I'll be back. Are you comfortable?' She plumped up his pillows in the time-honoured fashion.

'I'm fine. They've stuffed me with drugs. It slows me down but it takes away the pain, except when I laugh too much.' He chuckled again.

Dido smiled as she walked back to the desk. She was surprised at how delighted she was to see the old man again. There were a few rare people one met in life who were truly life-enhancers, and Perry was undoubtedly one of those. The atmosphere in his immediate vicinity had a lift and euphoria about it. Even the sickest patients who came under his smiling influence seemed for a time relieved of their anxiety and fear. He was a joy to have on the ward and Dido felt her own spirits rise.

Staff Nurse Julie Williams greeted her in a distracted manner. She was hurriedly writing up the last of her notes in the Kardex.

'Oh, hello, Di. We've been almost as busy as you seemed to be last night.'

'I suppose you heard about the dramas. How is Mr Manton?'

'He's out of his coma and the diabetes is responding to treatment. Dr Dauntcey decided to keep him in that side ward, so we're still responsible for nursing him. Apparently TB isn't as infectious as it was once thought to be. Although, as he's excreting tubercle bacilli, we have to be gowned, gloved and masked.' Dido smile wryly and Julie Williams looked at her closely and then continued, 'I suppose before he was formally diagnosed you were aspirating him without wearing a mask?'

Dido nodded. 'Mm, but I'm young and healthy. I don't expect to pick up anything from my patients. I've dealt with deadlier infections before.' Then, changing the subject, she asked, 'Have the tests for Mr Milsom's endocarditis come back?'

'Just in the nick of time. The X-ray this morning showed a slightly enlarged heart. Dr Dauntcey thought he was in incipient heart failure. Then, just as he was about to prescribe a blind course of drugs, the lab rang through. The bug's a penicillin-sensitive streptococcus and so Mr Milsom's on two mega units four-hourly.'

'That's administered through the drip, of course. Well, it's a small comfort to him that he's saved the discomfort of four-hourly mega-injections.'

Dido looked across to John Milsom's bed where he lay, less pale now and, incredibly, feeling well enough to listen to the radio. She had left him last night really sick and feverish. Dido thought what a relief it must be to Dr Dauntcey to be able to treat him at last, to have had his conservative policy proved correct.

Staff Nurse Williams consulted her notes again. 'We've discharged Mr Stiller. I'm afraid the Neurology department found his visually evoked response abnormal enough for Dr Dauntcey to be pretty certain in diagnosing multiple sclerosis. They'll get him back to Neurology Outpatients in a week or so when the results of the CSF analysis are known.'

'Oh dear. How did he take the news?' Dido was genuinely concerned.

'Well, Dr Dauntcey was extremely good in his explanation of the disease. He said it was relatively common. He was careful to stress that it didn't inevitably lead to the wheelchair—in fact, he said, a significant proportion of MS sufferers remained well and retained unrestricted mobility into middle and old age.'

Dido was grateful to James Dauntcey for managing to be both truthful and sensitive. He was a complex mixture of qualities and passions and the enigma of his character drew Dido's thoughts back to him time and time again. But with such reluctance—why, she did not even like the man much!

Julie Williams' voice cut through her wondering. 'Results on the clotting screen of Mr Manetti's blood came through too. Platelet count and prothrombin time are normal, so we went ahead with the liver biopsy. Results in four days' time.'

Dido looked across at his jolly face, surprisingly cheerful considering he had been without alcohol for nearly three days.

'Are you really managing to keep Mr Manetti off the booze? He looks so happy!'

Dido laughed as she spoke and Julie Williams frowned slightly. 'Well, we think we've vetted everything that's come in from outside. Unless he's got hold of the doctors' supplies.' They both giggled.

'I suppose that liver biopsy means we have to observe him frequently in case of internal bleeding? No wonder you've been so busy,' Dido said sympathetically. Then, looking across to where Peregrine Salmon sat, a book on his knees, she said, 'I've already met your new admission. He says it's his ticker. What's the official diagnosis?'

'He's got crescendo angina. He can't get out of bed without chest pain. I'm afraid it's extremely serious. He's had an electro-cardiograph and chest X-ray. We've done the usual blood tests.'

'I suppose as he's in here rather than surgical he's been deemed unsuitable for operation,' Dido said, her heart heavy with the knowledge that he was unlikely to live another year.

'You're right. Given his age and the presence of generalised arterial disease, an operation's unlikely. Dr Dauntcey has prescribed beta blockers and calcium antagonists and a little sedation, although he's so calm and philosophical he hardly needs it.'

'He's a fantastic old gentleman. I nursed him when I was a student. He really lifts the atmosphere on the ward.'

'I'll be off now. Hope you have a quiet night, Di.' Julie Williams tidied away the Kardex and picked up her bag. 'Oh, by the way, Dr Dauntcey said to tell you he may pop in tonight. He's in the hospital to see some other patient. He never seems to sleep.'

Julie disappeared through the ward swing doors on her way home to supper and a night out with her boyfriend, a radiographer called Sven.

As she prepared the drugs trolley, Dido wondered what private life, if any, Dr Dauntcey managed to squeeze in between his working days and nights. No wonder the woman in his life had been so angered by the demands of his work. Was she still with him? Or was he now with someone new? No one seemed to know anything personal about this most private man. There was gossip galore about his working life, about decisive diagnoses, intolerance of inefficiency, his devastating effect on the young women who worked with him, his appetite for work and daunting perfectionism, but not one whisper about his domestic arrangements.

All anyone knew was that he was probably titled and lived in Belgravia in a house big enough for a Victorian-sized family and a full complement of servants.

Dido did her drugs round, ending at the bedside of Perry Salmon.

'Can I see what you've been drawing?' Dido asked as she approached with his drugs.

'Of course, pet,' he replied and he held out the pad, on which was a full-page sketch of the ward with, in the foreground, a completely recognisable portrait of herself with her arm extended as if in welcome.

'Why, that's lovely!' Dido exclaimed, looking closer. She could recognise all the patients too, and there was Julie Williams' backview just as she went off duty. 'How are you feeling?' Dido put her hand on his arm and sat on the chair beside his bed.

'Oh, I'm just fine. But listen, pet,' he put his hand over hers and looked intently into her eyes, 'I've got something important to say and I'm telling you because I know you'll take me seriously.'

'I'm listening,' Dido said quietly.

'If anything happens to me, I don't want them messing about trying to revive me. I don't want any operations. I'm seventy-four, I've had a good life, and since my beloved Clemmie died it's not been the same.' He smiled, meeting Dido's eyes directly with his own surprisingly youthful gaze. 'I've had a marvellous life, but since she's gone I've been like a boat without a sail, my force and direction lost. I'm quite happy to accept my race is run.'

Dido nodded. She knew so many old people who approached death with the same philosophy and she believed that their wishes should be respected as far as possible.

'I knew you'd understand,' Perry said and patted her hand, his handsome old face relaxed and smiling.

'I do understand and sympathise and I'll mention it to Dr Dauntcey, who's ultimately responsible for your care,' Dido said with an affectionate lilt in her voice.

'That Dr Dauntcey, he's a good chap, pet. He's strong and courageous and good. You couldn't do better than him, my dear.' Perry smiled an innocent smile into the middle distance.

'What on earth do you mean, Mr Salmon?' She addressed him formally, startled at his suggestion of any personal connection between James Dauntcey and herself.

'Oh nothing, just that you couldn't have a better chap to work for,' he replied lightly, but then threw her the wickedest grin and with his forefinger gave the side of his large, patrician nose the most gentle of taps in a thoroughly knowing gesture. 'Just remember, I know you well—and I know what's good for you.'

'Oh, fiddlesticks!' Dido said, exasperated. 'You're an old romantic who'd read anything soppy into even the most businesslike relationship.'

'I may be an old romantic,' he retorted, 'but it's the best way to be. You wring the most happiness out of life that way, and I hope you'll follow my example.'

Dido stood up and looked at her watch. 'It's time you were asleep,' she said bossily. 'Now take your drugs and shut your eyes. I want to see you bright and breezy tomorrow morning.'

'Then I'm not taking the sedatives, those little yellow ones. I'm quite sedate enough.'

'Well, I'm not going to force-feed you them,' Dido said as she smiled another dazzlingly sweet smile. 'Sleep well, Perry.'

Dido walked slowly back to her desk. Her last patient, Sam Manton, needed his drugs. She donned a sterile gown, gloves and mask and pushed the trolley through to the side ward where he lay in isolation.

'Hello, Mr Manton,' Dido said quietly and as he opened his eyes she introduced herself. 'I'm Staff Nurse Alexander. I'm glad to see you recovering so well. I've just come to give you your drugs.'

He gave her a weak smile. 'Please call me Sam. I'm feeling better, thanks, Nurse. I can't tell you how good it is to be in a clean warm bed.'

Dido's heart went out to him when she thought how luxurious hospital accommodation must seem to him after sleeping rough, or at best managing to beg a narrow bed in the men's hostel down the road.

She took his wrist to count his pulse. It was still fast but improved, and his blood pressure was recovering, although still low. The meningitis would be responsible for that, Dido thought to herself.

'You're coming along well, Sam.' Dido patted his arm. 'Now here are your tablets.' She tipped his head forward to enable him to wash the pills down with a drink of water.

'I'm afraid this drug has to be injected into your bottom. Can you roll over onto your side?' Dido helped him to shift his position carefully so as not to dislodge the drip attached to his arm. She injected the streptomycin into the gluteus maximus muscle and then helped Sam roll onto his back again. 'Not a whimper, well done,' she smiled down at him.

'Nurse, anything is bearable as long as I've got a warm

bed and three meals a day. This is paradise indeed!' Sam chuckled.

Dido had to laugh too. 'It's nice to be so appreciated.' Then she picked up the fluid balance chart from the hook by the door and entered the two mouthfuls of water he had just had with his pills. His catheter had been removed but they were still monitoring his fluid intake and collecting his urine. Dido put the sheet back on the hook and returned to his bedside.

'You'll be off the drip tomorrow and we'll be sticking needles into you instead. Now, have the physiotherapists been along today to thump your back and give you breathing exercises?'

'Yes,' he grinned, 'two jolly girls. I felt as if I'd been duffed up by a band of yobos after they'd finished with me!'

'Good, that means they're doing their job properly. They'll be back tomorrow.'

'Lawd luv-a-duck! Perhaps I'm better off at the hostel.' And his laughter cracked up in a fit of coughing. Dido was grateful for her mask and gown as she handed him the sputum pot for him to spit into.

She plumped up his pillows and turned off the bed light. 'I hope you sleep well, Sam. If you want anything at all in the night please ring.' She pointed to the bell beside his bed. Dido walked to the door and hung up her gown. As she left the side ward she stripped off her mask and gloves and threw them into the incinerator bin.

She walked slowly back into the peaceful ward, her desk lamp casting a glow at the centre. She sat at the desk and filled in the Kardex, noting which patients were due for which treatment and when. As she pondered the case of John Milsom and the abatement of his fever since they had been able to treat him with antibiotics, Dido's attention was caught by a restless movement in one of the far beds. She peered through the dim light and saw the old artist's eyes looking back at her.

Walking to his bedside, she took his pale hand. 'Are you all right? Do you want something to help you sleep?'

'I'm OK, pet. I didn't mean to disturb you.'

'But that's just what I'm here for. We can't let routine get in the way of our caring for patients.' She laughed softly.

'I was just thinking about Clemmie. She was a wonderful woman, so beautiful and warm. A bit like you when she was younger,' and he squeezed her hand. 'I do miss her, now she's gone.'

'You're lucky to have had such a happy relationship,' Dido said, brushing his white hair from his forehead.

'It's partly luck, partly hard work and partly belief, my duck. I *believed* in our love and that helped us through the bad times and the dull times. But I was lucky to have chosen such a girl. She was a real good'un. That's my advice to you, pet. Get yourself a good'un and then work hard and go on believing.'

As he shifted postion, Dido noticed a spasm of pain contort his face. 'Perry, where's the pain?' she said calmly.

'I'm fine. Don't worry yourself about me,' he said cheerily, but the vein on his temple stood out in warning of the strain he was under.

'I'm not worrying myself. I just want to know where it hurts.' Dido's voice was firm. She had stood up and was leaning over him, willing him to look her in the face and tell her the truth.

'Well, if I tell you, remember your promise. No messing, no investigations.'

'I didn't promise; but I'll certainly let Dr Dauntcey

know your feelings. Now, show me where the pain is.'

The old man winced and closed his eyes, placing his open hands on his upper abdomen. 'It's bellyache here, and through to my back.'

'Let me just feel your legs.' Dido pulled up the covers from the foot of the bed and was shocked to find how cold his feet were.

Peregrine Salmon nodded. 'I can't feel them properly. I think they're cold,' he said calmly.

'They *are* cold. I'll be back in a moment.' Dido, her heart leaden with the implications of his fresh symptoms, walked briskly to the phone and asked the switchboard to bleep Dr Russell Brady.

She walked back to where Peregrine Salmon lay, peaceful but all at once deathly pale. 'Dr Brady will be with us in a minute,' she said, tucking the blankets in at the foot of bed.

'I know it's serious, pet. There's no need to beat about the bush. After all, it is my life . . . and my death,' he added softly.

'I know, Perry. You don't need to worry. We'll keep nothing from you. Now, tell me, is the pain bearable? I can't give you anything until Dr Brady's seen you.'

'Course it's bearable,' he said, mustering some vehemence. 'Pain in the gut's nothing like as bad as pain in the head. Nothing could be as nasty as the earache I used to get as a child.' And he managed a brave chuckle.

The ward doors banged and Russell Brady walked rapidly up to meet Dido. She had drawn the curtains around the old man's bed and talked quietly, out of his earshot.

'Sounds ominous,' Russell said as Dido related the fresh symptoms. 'Right, I'd better examine him and take some blood.' Having been carpeted the night before for not being conscientous enough, Russell Brady was going to take no chances. He sent a sample of blood off to the lab for analysis; he had to rule out acute inflammation of the pancreas. And in a separate bottle he sent some blood for cross-matching in case a transfusion was to prove necessary.

Both he and Dido were almost sure that Peregrine Salmon was suffering a leakage from an abdominal aortic aneurysm that was likely to rupture at any time. They knew that an attempt to surgically repair the leak would almost surely kill him, just as certainly as his condition would.

'I'll bleep Frank,' Dr Brady said, realising he had to involve his senior registrar in any such major decision.

Dido was back by Perry's side. He was holding her hand now, still not complaining at the pain and seemingly unafraid. He was talking about his days as a student at the Royal College of Art. It was an increasing effort for him to speak.

'They were lovely days, after the first war. We were the lucky generation, we'd escaped death. We saw our elder brothers and friends go away and never return. We felt that every year of life given to us was a gift.' As he spoke, his voice almost a whisper, Dido stroked his hand, cradling it between the two of hers.

She heard the curtains part behind her but continued to listen to the old artist's story. Then, glancing up, her gaze met the glittering blue eyes of James Dauntcey, looking down at her with a curious, gentle expression in his face, his lips smiling slightly. Dido was seeing him in a quite different light and it took her aback.

'Hello, Perry.' Immediately his attention was switched to the patient. 'Let's see what's troubling you.' Dr Dauntcey prepared to gently palpate his abdomen.

Peregrine Salmon whispered between clenched teeth, 'It's good to see you, Doc. I've given my last orders to your beautiful Staff Nurse here. So you'd better heed what she says.' His face, so pale and benign he seemed almost to have the head of a waxen saint, managed a ghost of a smile.

'I always heed what she says,' Dr Dauntcey said quietly as he put his fingers on the old man's groin to take his femoral pulses. He turned to Frank Berenson and said briefly, 'Femoral pulse absent on left, weak on right.'

Dido knew that meant that the circulation to his legs was cut off by the bleeding in his abdomen. That things were very serious indeed.

Then, turning to Perry, Dr Dauntcey said, 'We'll give you something for the pain. I'll be back to see you in a minute.' He took Dr Berenson's arm and together they departed through the drawn curtains. 'Staff Alexander, could you come too? Dr Brady will look after Mr Salmon,' he called over his shoulder.

The two doctors and Dido stood in the circle of light round her desk.

'Well, I'm afraid it's an abdominal aortic aneurysm. It's obviously seeping and likely to rupture. What would you do, Frank?' James Dauntcey asked.

Frank Berenson looked up from his notes, a troubled frown on his brow. 'I know he's old and his heart condition makes it very dodgy, but I wouldn't want to rule out an operation. I would hate to just leave him.'

James Dauntcey turned his darkly handsome face to Dido. He was concentrating and the twitching muscle in his square jaw was highlighted by the glow from her lamp. 'Staff, what's your opinion? I know you're privy to the patient's wishes.'

Dido looked steadily into his eyes, her fine-spun hair caught in the light like a luminous veil around her pale, heart-shaped face.

'I think it would be a mistake to operate. I don't believe he would survive the anaesthetic and, given his strong request not to undergo surgery, I think we should nurse him, treat his pain and leave him be.' Dido looked down at her hands and thought what a terrible decision it was, and for a medical team, trained to act to save lives, how difficult it was to decide to do nothing. She looked back at Dr Dauntcey, whose gaze seemed distant and preoccupied.

'Given his wishes, I'd rather he died as peacefully as possible, rather than on the operating table. I think I agree with you, Staff. Given how seriously arteriosclerotic he is, he wouldn't last the operation. I think we'll give him something to settle him. Diamorphine—can you do that, Staff?' He glanced again at Dido, who was strangely moved by the concern in his eyes. 'I'll come back with you now to see him.' And as he took her elbow gently in his hand, Dido was aware of a melting in her limbs, an unexpectedly Victorian desire to swoon in his arms, to be held against his hard warm body and kept safe from the world.

But reality was different. Dr Dauntcey drew apart the curtains around Peregrine Salmon's bed and held them for Dido to pass through. The old man lay deathly pale, his eyes closed.

'Perry.' Dr Dauntcey touched his shoulder and his eyelids fluttered open. 'Has Dr Brady got rid of most of the pain for you?' His white head nodded and he smiled as Dr Dauntcey continued, 'We're not going to operate.

I quite agree with you on that, so Staff is going to give you something to settle you down.' Dr Dauntcey waited for a few seconds to allow the old man a chance to ask him any further questions and then left without saying goodbye.

Dido returned to Perry's bedside with a syringe pack and the Diamorphine. There was a tearful lump deep in her chest which she had to keep under control. She had had many patients die and there was a sadness each time, but tonight, with this singular old man who was like a member of her own family she had known for years, she was not ready yet to let go.

'You did well there, pet.' His words were barely discernible now, but still had a timbre of humour about them. 'I knew I could depend on you.'

Dido smiled and took his hand. 'Of course you can depend on me. Now, I just have to give you this injection in your thigh.' As she leaned over the old man he looked up at her, his eyes surprisingly brilliant and youthful.

'Listen, pet. One last thing you've got to do for me. Tell me the truth.' Dido met his clear look without embarrassment and nodded. 'How much longer?' As he spoke, Dido knew she could not prevaricate. He had asked her to respect his need for the truth.

'Not long. A major blood-vessel is bleeding into your stomach. We'll give you morphine for the pain. It may make you a little bit drowsy. It's not unpleasant,' she added quietly.

Suddenly the tension between them was broken and he gave an impish smile. 'How do you know?' he whispered.

Dido tweaked his nose and said, 'A little fairy at the bottom of my garden told me.'

'Well, if you'll stay with me I'll tell you if she was right.'

'Of course I'll stay,' Dido said as she gently pulled up the blankets. She sat stroking his hair and listening to his breathing becoming shallower, all the while keeping the tears from springing into her eyes.

She was startled from her painful reverie by Perry's whispered words. 'You're right, pet. I'm on a cloud floating towards a rainbow. I'm sure Clemmie's waiting for me there.' His words faded away.

Dido felt a tremendous tiredness overcome her. She sat there, oblivious to the passage of time, in a daze of fatigue and sadness, stroking the old artist's hand until it grew cold. Tears smarted at the back of her eyes but somehow did not fall. But just as she felt herself sinking with fatigue, Dido found herself lifted bodily to her feet.

A voice whispered in her ear, 'You've been marvellous. You've done all you could for him. Now come with me, you need a good strong cup of coffee to revive you.'

Dido looked up, past the dark suit with the stethoscope protruding from the pocket, past the sober tie and the spotless white shirt, past the firm, bristle-shadowed chin and the full warm mouth, up to those mesmeric blue eyes, their expression softened now with compassion.

They sat in Sister's office while James Dauntcey made the coffee. 'I owe you an apology for yesterday,' he said, intent on pouring the water into the machine. 'Russell Brady told me today that you had suspected TB and he had dismissed your suggestion. May I offer my congratulations on being so intelligent and observant and my apologies for not asking you for your version of events.'

Dido was so surprised to have the great Dr Dauntcey apologise to her, and in such a formal way, that she

almost felt she ought to incline her head in regal acceptance. He looked up at her and then glanced quickly away
as if the intimacy of this small room and the power of
attraction between them made it far too dangerous for
their eyes to meet more than fleetingly.

'The more I see you, the more I admire you. Your
efficiency and professionalism is not at all at the expense
of your compassion and humanity. You're a remarkable
young woman.' Almost against his will it seemed, his
eyes were drawn to her face as if by an irresistible force.

Dido was so full of emotion she gazed back at him, her
gold-flecked eyes brilliant with unshed tears, and she
marvelled at the sweetness and vulnerability in his expression.

She could not analyse for that moment the emotions
that surged through her, the full implication of his words
or the gentleness in his face. When he held out his hand
for her coffee cup, all she could think to do was to put her
hand there instead, and they sat like that for many
moments, hands touching, eyes drinking deeply, each of
the other.

'Dido, Dido . . .' he said her name so reverently, so
quietly, she was not sure whether she heard his voice or
read her name on his lips. It was the first time he had ever
used her name in her company and she felt her heart turn
over with the thrilling intimacy of the moment.

Suddenly, a sharp knock on the door broke their
meditation. Their hands sprung apart. Dido's pale cheek
flushed pink as if they were lovers caught in an illicit
embrace. Frank Berenson popped his head round the
door.

'Sorry, sir, but there's an emergency on Hartland.
Can you come now?'

'Of course.' James Dauntcey stood up, tall and impressive and detached. 'Thanks for the coffee, Staff,' he said brusquely, but his fingers lightly brushed her cheek as he swept out of the door.

CHAPTER SIX

'WHAT ON earth have you been up to? You look like you've won the pools, been dated by Robert Redford and signed up to star in his next film, all on the same day!' Millie gazed aghast at her friend. The last time she had seen Dido was the previous morning, when her friend had crawled back from night duty at the hospital, exhausted and demoralised, ready to give up nursing for good.

Millie had done her best to cheer Dido up yesterday morning but had then spent most of her free moments on the ward that day worrying about her. Dido was a marvellous nurse, intelligent and warm-hearted, un-ruffled—apart from her redhead's temper—and calmly philosophical. It was unlike her to get so depressed and unthinkable that she would give up nursing.

Millie had begun to wonder if the sheer hard work, the unremitting responsibility for people's lives, the long unsociable hours, were beginning seriously to under-mine her friend's excellent temperament. It happened to enough good nurses. But not to Dido, Millie hoped fervently.

But all these worries and speculations seemed to be wildly unfounded as Millie faced the radiant apparition of her friend. Dido had just arrived home from the hospital. Instead of fatigue etching its familiar shadows under her brows, those glorious eyes sparkled with a brilliance which could only be a sign of extreme happiness. Her fine skin, flushed by the cold, was gleaming with a translucency which seemed to come from within.

Dido walked slowly into the room, her red-gold hair blown free of its braiding, shimmering in unruly waves round her face. For a moment she appeared not to have heard Millie's exclamation but seemed to be tuned in to some other wavelength.

'Di, are you all right?' Millie had walked towards her and uttered a slightly nervous giggle. If she did not know her friend better she might have suspected her of being high on drugs.

'I'm fine! I am brilliantly, wonderfully fine.' Dido was dancing around, swooping and pirouetting like a small girl alone in her room. Millie was still not reassured. This was odd behaviour from someone as level-headed and unsusceptible as Staff Nurse Dido Alexander.

'You certainly look brilliantly, wonderfully fine, but I'd be grateful if you'd share your secret with me. I'd give anything to be so energised after ten hours of night duty!'

Dido came to a graceful halt, her arms, still draped in her hospital cape, outstretched, hands pointing delicately, in the pose remembered from schoolgirl ballet classes.

'I wish I knew myself! I've never felt like this before.' She laughed as she met Millie's puzzled eyes. 'I think it's just that I've fallen head over heels in love.'

'Well then, a good cold shower's what you need my girl!' Millie said in mock sternness, pointing towards the bathroom.

'I know it sounds ridiculous. But there it is.' Dido was serious now, standing in the sitting-room in front of Millie while the pale winter sun bathed them in its tepid warmth.

'Well, you'd better tell me who the lucky chap is,' Millie said unenthusiastically.

Dido was not at all hurt by her friend's reaction to the news. Millie had supported her loyally through the trauma of the break-up of her last relationship. She had suffered with Dido and Dido knew she was loath to have either of them go through that all again. Besides, she thought, Millie is a realist, always suspicious of the idea of 'falling in love'. And so Dido approached, with some apprehension, the revelation of exactly who was the focus of such folly.

'You don't really know him,' she hedged.

'Oh, come off it, Di! It's someone at the hospital, I know that much. Come on, tell your old friend.'

'All right then, but promise you won't be cynical?' Dido took a deep breath. 'I'm in love with Dr James Dauntcey.' Even as she spoke, she was alarmed by the boldness and unfamiliarity of the words. Dido repeated them silently to herself, savouring the full meaning of her statement.

Millie took a few seconds to understand exactly what her friend had said. She slowly blanched. 'You're not serious?' As Dido dumbly nodded she continued, 'But half the female population of St Ben's is in love with Dr Dauntcey. How do you know that you're any different?' Mille spoke gently, not wanting to hurt with her blunt words, and Dido was taken aback for a moment.

Of course, she knew in the back of her mind that a man as good-looking and successful as Dr Dauntcey would attract women, but Dido had not given it much thought. Somehow, being on night duty and very busy had insulated her from the usual rounds of gossip and speculation. Millie was right, she thought for a heart-broken moment. What gave her any reason to think that

Dr Dauntcey would see her as anything more than a pretty and besotted girl?

Then the memory of those revelatory moments in the office, when he had spoken her name and looked at her with such gentleness and longing, revived Dido's spirit. It *was* real. She was not indulging in wishful delusions. Something unique and precious existed between them and that something was love.

But Millie was still playing devil's advocate. 'You know nothing about him. You don't even know if he's married or not. Please be careful, Dido,' she pleaded, her face contorted with anxiety.

'All I know is what I feel. And feelings can't be denied. I can't stop myself loving him, so I might as well trust in him and see where it leads.' Dido was quiet and confident. She knew there was no way she could pretend that night had not happened, pretend her heart had not turned over and beat now to a different rhythm, in tune with the heart of another. She could not turn back the clocks. She had to follow her heart.

Dido stood in front of her friend, surprised by her own emotional confidence. Until a few weeks ago she had believed herself immune to falling in love again—and yet here she was, expressing romantic concepts as if they were life-long beliefs.

Then Dido remembered Peregrine Salmon and she smiled. It had been that wise old man who had declared that Dr James Dauntcey and Staff Nurse Dido Alexander were just made for each other, and indeed his death had brought them together. She thanked him from the bottom of her heart.

'What are you smiling for?' Millie asked her, grinning despite herself, for Dido's joy was catching.

'I was just thinking about an old patient, an artist we

had in yesterday. He was talking about love and he said to me "find a good 'un and then work at it and go on believing", and I think he's right.' Dido's eyes shone with fervour again.

'I think he's right too, but we have yet to see if you've found yourself that good 'un. Frankly, a doctor—and possibly a married doctor at that—looks much more like a bad 'un to me!' Millie said emphatically, although her infectious grin took some of the force from her words.

There was no disputing Millie's logic, but Dido knew, in some inexplicable way, that James Dauntcey had been sincere that night, that he could not have looked at her in such a way, with his heart in his eyes, if he had been emotionally committed elsewhere.

'Millie, I know in principle you're right. But I have to trust my instincts and they tell me that he is true and trustworthy.'

Millie smiled and took her friend's arm. 'Well, I hope your faith is rewarded. You give so much happiness to others you deserve a good measure in return.' Then she looked at her watch. It was almost time for her to go. 'You've got a couple of days off now before you're back on days, so let's go out for a drink tonight. We could try that new wine bar opposite the hospital. Get some sleep now, see you later.' And Millie put on her coat, picked up her bag and ran quickly down the stairs to the street.

Dido was too elated to sleep. She had two days off, a fact that would have filled her with delight a few weeks ago but now was roundly regretted for keeping her away from the one person she wanted to be near. She had forgotten about the obsessive quality of being in love, of wanting to be in his presence, gaze on his face, know everything of his past and share his future.

She wanted to broadcast her discovery to everyone, longed to call her mother, tell her friends, but a slight superstition kept her from picking up the phone. After all, what could she say? 'I'm in love with a handsome consultant. Yes, I'm pretty sure he feels the same for me. No, he hasn't exactly said so. I just know, that's all . . .' Dido knew it would just sound like a crush, something susceptible nurses harbour for personable doctors as commonly as drains harbour germs. No, she would wait until she had something more concrete to tell. She was not keen to have her family and friends think she had fallen into the trap of a one-sided affair.

Dido walked over to the mirror in the hall and gazed at her reflection as if it belonged to another. Her eyes shone with amusement and excitement at some secret knowledge. She pushed back from her face the mass of red-gold hair. Little fronds curled at her forehead and by her cheekbones and the rest cascaded over her shoulders, almost to her waist.

As a little girl, Dido had hated her hair, hated its waviness and its colour. She had longed for straight black hair, like her best friend, Susanna's. As she had grown into a teenager she had taken to ironing it between two sheets of paper in an attempt to curb its exuberance. She had not been bold enough to dye it black but had soaked it in tea to try and tone down the reddish gold, which shone like a flame and earned her the nickname 'hothead' at school. Her grandmother had tut-tutted and scolded, 'You're perfect as God made you. Straight hair wouldn't suit you and black would make you look ill!'

Dido had felt then that fate had been particularly unkind to lumber her with the double indignity of both red and curly hair. Only since she had started nursing,

and grown up, had she come to agree with her grandmother and appreciate the physical characteristics with
which she had been blessed. As she stood in the hall, her
eyes sparkling and her glorious hair making a dramatic
foil for her fine, fair skin, Dido was thankful with all her
heart for her own individual beauty.

Although she felt vibrant and thoroughly awake,
Dido knew she needed to get some sleep that morning
and then go to bed again that evening to get herself back
into the new routine of day duty. A long, luxurious bath
would help the sleep process, she thought as she turned
on the taps and poured a big dollop of her expensive bath
oil into the churning water. Submerged up to her neck in
the warm, fragrant water, Dido's brain and body suc-
cumbed to a delicious torpor. She could barely muster
the energy to pull out the bath plug.

At last she was tucked up in bed and blissfully unaware of anything but a sunny dream, starring James
Dauntcey. She was on a paradise island with him, but
inexplicably dressed in winter clothes, complete with
boots and coat, while he was wearing only swimming
trunks. Dido longed to go swimming but could not see a
way round the problem of her clothes. James Dauntcey
emerged from the aquamarine ocean, glistening with
water, and slowly walked towards her, his eyes as blue as
the sea. He kissed her. How Dido trembled as his lips
brushed her neck, her earlobe, traced their butterfly
path across her cheek and settled warmly, hungrily, on
her quivering mouth.

At this point an uneasy thought intruded into Dido's
dream state. Into her fertile unconscious crept the cold
logic of her conscious mind—perhaps this ecstasy was
only a dream? But Dido did not want to wake yet. She
could not bear to let this dream slip away. Surfacing

from the kiss, she clung to her dream lover and whispered that she wanted to join him in the sea. With joy she felt her body lighten and open towards the sun as he slowly removed her coat, her blouse, her skirt. Trembling with anticipation and desire, she felt his warm touch on her shoulder as his hands released her from the bondage of her clothing and the sun's rays and his dark appreciative gaze warmed her to the core.

With panic, Dido realised the dream was fading, losing focus and definition. She wanted so badly to reach that warm, inviting sea, wrapped in the arms of her lover, but she knew she could not conjure it back.

Her brain sprang into wakefulness as refreshed as if she had actually been away to that paradise isle. Dido looked at her watch. Two thirty in the afternoon, a good time to wake up if she was going to try and get back into the habit of sleeping at night.

She sat on the edge of her bed, savouring the dream, longing to make it reality. Then, shaking herself out of the romantic reverie, Dido slowly started to get dressed. There was a hundred and one small chores to be done and she knew she would feel burdened until she had tackled them, so she donned her jeans and an old jumper and started with the washing.

That evening after supper, she changed into an indigo mohair jumper and a pair of flattering navy wool trousers and went with Millie to the new wine bar, Grapevine, opposite the hospital. As they walked into the pretty interior they were greeted by other nurses and doctors who were enjoying a few drinks or a light meal after coming off duty, or for those doctors with bleepers, a little conviviality while on call.

Dido led the way to a little table by the open fire and she and Millie started discussing a particularly interesting patient who had been admitted to Cardiothoracics that day.

'Talking shop again, girls? Can we join you?' Dido looked up, surprised to see Frank Berenson and his houseman, Russell Brady, grinning down at them.

. 'I haven't seen you for ages, Frank. How are you?' Dido said laughing, for in fact Frank had been called in the previous night to give an opinion on Mr Salmon. But certainly she had not seen him socially, nor had a chance to talk, for a long time.

'I'm tired, Di, awfully tired. Come away on a sunlit holiday with me. It's the only way I'll ever recover my legendary strength!' He held her hand to his chest in a mock gesture of romantic pleading.

'I only seem to get there in my dreams. But wouldn't it be nice to see the sun again,' Dido said longingly.

Russell sat down next to Millie, almost unrecognisable without his white coat. He leaned across towards Dido and said, 'I hope our superman consultant apologised to you over Mr Manton's TB. I should have admitted full liability the moment my cover was blown. I'm sorry, Di, but I was absolutely shattered and old High-and-Mighty didn't exactly give either of us a chance to open our mouths.' He sat back with a sigh.

'Yes, he did apologise. Thanks, Russell,' Dido said briefly, praying that Millie had the good sense not to say anything about there being more than apologies passing between them.

Luckily, Russell was continuing his own train of thought. 'We've had a rather dramatic run of night duties while you've been in charge, Di. I'm just hoping now you're on days again I'll be able to get some sleep. I'm knackered!'

'Ooh, you poor doctors. Both so exhausted it's all you

can do to drag yourself down to the Grapevine every night!' Millie said, giggling as she was playfully cuffed by Frank.

Russell nudged her. 'I suppose you angelic nurses never complain of tiredness or aching feet,' and as both Dido and Millie looked wide-eyed and slowly shook their heads, he snorted, 'Not half!'

'I'll look forward to seeing more of you now you're back on days,' Frank said quietly to Dido, a serious and affectionate expression on his face.

Dido smiled. 'Yes, I'm looking forward to getting back to a slightly more normal routine,' she answered, evading the romantic interest implicit in his words.

At that moment Dido looked up to see a group enter the wine bar, at the centre of which was the unmistakable figure of James Dauntcey. He had not seen her and she immediately turned her head away, her cheeks flushed with the memory of her dream still so vividly in her mind. What a fool! she scolded herself, reacting as if the dream images had been real.

Dido hoped the others in her group had not noticed her confusion and she turned calmly to Frank, determined to start up the conversation again.

'Have you booked your holiday yet? You usually manage to fit in a couple of weeks skiing at this time of year.' But her eyes were drawn irresistibly back to the group of senior doctors talking and drinking at the bar.

How distinguished and handsome he looked standing there, laughing at something said, then elegantly putting his point of view, his long-fingered hands gesturing, then returning to hold his drink. Dido gazed at the tall, straight back, the broad shoulders jutting beneath his immaculate dark suit, the uniform for consultants but in

Dr Dauntcey's case, made to measure, hand-tailored and proclaiming its class in every inch of cloth.

Dido looked at Frank as he seriously answered her question, expanding on the relative merits of snow conditions in various ski resorts. Then her eyes strayed back to the man who had so infiltrated her very being that now he dominated her waking thoughts, even her dreams, and filled her with such longing that without him she felt incomplete.

As she gazed, Dido suddenly thought of practical Millie and her sceptical warnings. She watched Dr Dauntcey, relaxed amongst his peers, oblivious to her presence, and she wondered for a moment if she was deluding herself in thinking he could ever be interested in her, a young, inexperienced woman, merely a staff nurse.

As that doubt flickered into her head, Dido saw James Dauntcey turn and laugh into the eyes of the woman who stood at his elbow. He looked at his watch, appeared to ask her something, said his goodbyes to the group and then left in her company. Dido thought she recognised the woman as Dr Marie Walker, paediatrics registrar, a pretty, dark-haired woman whose chequered love-life was discussed avidly by the nurses in the canteen.

The incident did not shake her faith exactly, but it skimmed the cream off her elation. Dido still felt entirely committed in her love for Dr Dauntcey and in her heart of hearts she knew that her fleeting doubt was natural, yet unfounded. But that doubt had entered her head and could not be dismissed completely.

Dido turned to her friends. 'I'm rather tired. I think I'll turn in,' and, keen to disrupt the group as little as possible, she declined all offers to walk her home. 'I'll be fine. Thanks, anyway, but it's only a brisk ten minutes away.'

Dido ran most of the way home, not just to ensure her safety but because she felt she had to run to stop herself thinking and speculating. Within minutes she was home and by the time Millie returned, she was fast asleep.

The morning of her first day back on duty dawned clear and bright. Dido felt surprisingly tired, despite the fact she had slept away most of her two days off duty. Perhaps she had been overdoing things more than she had realised.

Dido had breakfast with Millie, although she could not face the egg and bacon her friend was tucking into so enthusiastically.

'Did you sleep all right? You look rather peaky, Di,' Millie said in between mouthfuls.

'Yes, not bad. I don't know why I feel so tired. Perhaps I've upset my biological time clock.' She laughed, for medicine could be said to be a career tailor-made to disrupt biological time clocks. She had lost count of how many times she was wide awake at three in the morning and dead to the world as the rest of the population were enjoying the midday sun. Dido had always felt that, in summer particularly, forcing herself to become a nocturnal animal was not altogether healthy. But then, caring for sick people was a full-time occupation and so it was not worth worrying about the effects on one's own health and well-being.

Together they walked to the hospital through busy streets, cold and bright in the morning sun. Dido felt the cold air revive her a bit. It certainly whipped some colour into her cheeks and added a sparkle to her eyes.

Millie was preoccupied and subdued. Dido glanced at her usually ebullient friend who was walking beside her, head down, her hands thrust deep into the pockets of her coat.

'It's all very well worrying about me, but you don't look too good yourself. What's up?' Dido asked her as casually as she could.

'Oh, I'm OK. It's just that I'd like to meet a nice chap. Not to fall madly in love with,' she added hastily. 'You know how suspicious I am of headlong love affairs, but just a special man to go places with and do things together would be nice.' Millie kicked disconsolately at an old cigarette carton that lay on the pavement.

'I know, Millie. But it'll happen, I'm certain of that.' Dido linked her arm through her friend's and Millie smiled in response.

'Of course you're right. And even if you weren't, there's nothing I can do about it.' She turned and looked Dido full in the face. 'Anyway, enjoy your love affair but don't lose your common sense. You're too special to be hurt like that again.'

They entered the main doors of the hospital and were enveloped in the familiar warmth and smell of disinfectant and ether. Millie turned left and waved as Dido walked briskly up to Millington ward. Pushing her way through the doors, she was pleased to see that her friend Anne Bradshaw had been on duty that night and would probably be handing over a shipshape ward.

'Gosh, Di, it's good to see you again. It always takes some getting used to, going back on nights again.'

'Have you had a quiet time?' Dido smiled, and then looked over Anne's shoulder as she riffled through the Kardex.

'It's been remarkably quiet, thank goodness.'

'The emergencies must wait until I'm on. My last two night duties were the busiest I've ever had!' Dido laughed ruefully, hoping the period of calm would continue through the day.

Anne smiled slyly up at Dido. 'Yes, I heard that Dr Dauntcey practically lived on the ward.'

Dido ignored Anne's explicit curiosity and laughed casually. 'It wasn't quite that bad. But we did seem to have more than our fair share of demanding cases. Have you got anyone new for me?' she enquired, changing the subject.

'Only one. Quite interesting really.' Anne looked over to the bed by the largest window where a young man lay bathed in sunshine. 'A Mr Billy Newton. With Elephant Man's Disease!'

When she saw Dido's eyes widen with concern, she added quickly, 'It's a mild form of neurofibromatosis. He's got the *cafe-au-lait* patches of skin pigmentation and a few benign tumours. He's in for observation and a few tests. Dr Dauntcey suspects there may be a neurofibroma in his spine, so he's due for a myelogram today.'

Dido realised the patient was watching them talking about him and so she walked slowly over to the bed and smiled down on the young man. 'Hello, Mr Newton, I'm Staff Nurse Alexander and I'll be on day duty while you're with us.' She met his eyes without embarrassment, even though his appearance was surprising and slightly bizarre. His face was irregular and lumpy, although not unpleasantly so, and his skin was pale except for the characteristic patches which spread from his cheeks like faded coffee stains.

He grinned up at her, a lopsided, friendly grin, and Dido noticed what humorous grey eyes he had.

'I'm fine, thanks, Staff. They really know how to lay on the de luxe treatment here. Makes a change from working, doesn't it?' As Dido returned to the desk where Annie was seated, the young man picked up his newspaper and resumed his reading.

Dido knew the tumours which characterised this inherited disorder would continue to appear and grow throughout his life. Hopefully they would all be benign, and luckily their growth would be slow. They could, however, grow so as to eventually distort his face beyond recognition. Dido felt a surge of sympathy for him; the human face was the most personal and expressive part of the external features of the body and its disfigurement affected most people more than the loss of a limb.

Anne Bradshaw gave her report on the progress of the remaining patients and then gathered her coat and her belongings and set off thankfully for bed.

Dido looked at her watch. She had half an hour before the consultant's round and she went through the Kardex system quickly to check again on each patient's progress. She did not want to seem ill-informed in front of the full team of senior doctors including, of course, James Dauntcey. The ward looked tidy and cheerful, beds neatly made, flowers brightening most of the bedsides and a determined sun filtering through the lofty windows.

Just as the doctors' arrival was imminent, Dido noticed a visitor slip through the ward doors and hurry to Mr Manetti's bedside. Dido marched up and firmly asked the middle-aged man to leave, for no visiting was allowed until the doctors' round had finished. As she turned on her heel she heard the crackle of crumpled paper and she returned to Mr Manetti's side.

'What have you got there, under the bedclothes?' she asked him coolly. He had alcoholic cirrhosis and they were being scrupulous about keeping him off alcohol, despite determined and ingenious efforts from his family and friends.

Mr Manetti beamed innocently up at her. 'Only the book I'm reading, Staff,' he said. But Dido had been nursing too long to be taken in by that. She deftly flicked back the bedclothes on the far side of his bed and, without any of the other patients being aware that she was doing anything other than straightening out the bed, she removed a brown paper packet.

'Ah, Staff, have a heart! I'll die without a drop or two. It's good medicine, that.'

'You'll die if you have any more drops of this,' she said sternly and made to carry the packet off to Sister's office. But before she could get there, the ward doors banged and three doctors, their white coat-tails flying out behind them, strode purposefully onto the ward.

Dido was slightly disconcerted to come unexpectedly face to face with James Dauntcey. She coloured faintly and his intensely blue eyes bored into her own, missing nothing.

'Good morning, Staff,' he said lightly. Frank Berenson and houseman Russell Brady greeted her more warmly.

Russell's eyes lit on the packet in Dido's hands, from which protruded the unmistakable top of a well-known brand of whisky.

'Have you been hitting the bottle again, Staff?' he said, laughing over-loudly at his own joke. Dr Dauntcey's dark brows knitted together in a slight frown. He did not care for Russell's familiarity with Dido.

Dido had coloured more deeply and cursed herself for having such a fair skin which broadcast every emotion.

'No, I've just had to confiscate it from Mr Manetti,'

she said with a defiant toss of her head—she did not care for Russell's over-familiarity either. Dido excused herself and went through to Sister's office where she locked the offending bottle in the cupboard.

When she returned to the ward all three doctors were standing round Mr Manetti's bed. Dido joined them in time to hear Dr Dauntcey outlining in emphatic terms to the patient just why it was so important that he should not drink.

As they turned away from the bed and moved out of his earshot, Dr Dauntcey said to Frank, Russell and Dido, 'The liver biopsy results showed typical alcoholic cirrhosis. We've taken him off Heminevrin and we've told him the worst. But in spite of that he seems remarkably cheerful. I'm afraid he'll probably go straight back on the hard stuff the moment he gets outside these doors. It's a common enough pattern.'

Dido looked from the patient's ruddy face to the darkly handsome features of the man she loved and said in a cool, professional tone of voice, 'It's possible he's been getting some of the hard stuff even while he's been within these doors. I'm afraid his friends and relatives may have managed to smuggle some through, despite our strict surveillance. Should we do a blood alcohol level test?'

'Good idea, Staff. Russell, could you see to that?' Dido and Dr Dauntcey were entirely correct and formal in their professional roles and Dido knew it had to be that way, but how she longed for some reassurance, some indication of how he felt.

Dr Dauntcey was reading the notes in his hands. Then, raising his head, he turned to Frank. 'Given these results, what prognosis would you give Mr Manetti?'

Frank lowered his voice. 'Not good, I'm afraid. It's a

progressive disease but at least, being alcohol related, if he stops drinking he shouldn't deteriorate as rapidly as if he had presented with ascites or jaundice. But you can never be certain. He does seem well. Perhaps he'll live more than five years, but I think he'd be lucky if he did.'

Dido had been watching Dr Dauntcey while Frank expounded his opinion on the prospects for Mr Manetti's cirrhosis. To her irritation, her heart had seemed to leap and flutter despite her attempts to keep it in check. Dido folded her hands across her waist to prevent them from involuntarily reaching out to touch his arm. Only once did James Dauntcey look up, and then he gazed straight into her eyes for a fleeting moment. But the expression on his face was intense and inscrutable, and quickly gone. There was nothing to indicate to Dido that she meant more to him than any efficient staff nurse on his ward.

'I agree with you, Frank.' He spoke reflectively, gazing towards the window where the winter sun still managed to palely illuminate the nearest beds. 'It's hard to give any definite prognosis as so many factors are involved. But I do think we should impress on the patient the importance of abstinence. Staff, perhaps you could contact Alcoholics Anonymous and see if they can offer him some support when he first leaves hospital. Oh, and I think a daily shot of Multivite while he's with us wouldn't be a bad idea. Would you see to that?' He looked over at Dido without a flicker of affection or intimacy in his blue eyes. It was Russell and Frank who winked at her, gave her fond smiles and stood close to her whenever they could.

Dido nodded. 'Yes, of course I'll see to that.' She began to wonder if Millie could not be right after all. Perhaps she was deluding herself? Perhaps the emotional strain of Peregrine Salmon's death, the lateness of the hour and the intimacy of the darkness had misled them both? Perhaps Dr Dauntcey was heartily regretting any indiscretion or intimacy of tone? Perhaps she herself had inflated a mere friendliness into heights of grand passion? These thoughts lingered miserably in Dido's mind. Even the fact that she had seen him leave the wine bar last night with a female colleague assumed sinister connotations.

As the consultant's round came to an end, Dido felt peculiarly tired and subdued. During their customary cup of coffee in Sister's office she barely contributed anything to the informal discussion of the cases they had just seen. Just as Dido thought the doctors had gone and she was alone, she was startled to see the dark figure of Dr Dauntcey at the door.

He stood there, so tall and lean in his tailored suit, his dark, almost black, hair emphasising the angular planes of his handsome face. Dido noticed his fine brown hands were clenched and she wondered what tensions he was controlling. His piercing gaze searched her face as if seeking reassurance, some message or sign.

Dido could not know that James Dauntcey, the cool, self-contained professional, was plagued with desire for her. His waking thoughts, even his dreams, were full of her. He longed to see her face but then, at the sight ot that translucent skin, the fine tip-tilted nose and her mesmerising cat's eyes meeting his gaze with seriousness and lack of guile, his longing to sweep her into his arms was almost too much to contain.

So it was that one of the most controlled of men stood in front of Dido, his hands clenched to prevent them reaching for her, loosening her glorious hair and crushing her warm, yielding body to his chest.

'Can I ring you tonight?' he said abruptly.

Dido's startled eyes met his for an instant and then looked back at the coffee cup in her hands. The atmosphere between them was so electric she felt to look longer would risk being burned. 'Yes, of course,' was all she could say.

Looking up again, she saw he had gone and her heart once more leapt with joy. He was serious. Her faith had been justified.

Dido's fatigue was temporarily washed away. She donned a gown, mask and gloves and went into the side ward to attend to Sam Manton, whose diabetes was fully under control now. His tuberculosis required long-term treatment and because of his circumstances and the risk that he would neglect his daily drug needs, they were all prepared to have him on the ward for weeks, even months.

As she entered the room, Dido was delighted to see the change in Sam. He had had his hair washed and cut, he was clean-shaven and the smiling face that greeted her seemed to have lost twenty years in the process.

'You look marvellous, Sam. How are you feeling?' she asked him as she prepared a syringe containing soluble insulin.

'I feel marvellous, thanks, Nurse. Never better. Do you think when I leave here, all spruced up and full of good food, that I'll find a good woman to marry me?' He winked at her.

'I wouldn't be at all surprised, Sam. You'll just have to keep an eye out for her. But you'll have to look after yourself too, you know. No more neglecting to take your drugs and getting ill again.'

She injected the insulin into his thigh and then pulled the bedclothes up and tucked them in. 'I'll be back later.

I must get on with the rest of my patients now. Have you got enough to read?' And as Sam Manton nodded and held up a lurid-looking paperback, Dido grimaced and laughed.

Back on the main ward, she was just about to go and minister to Mr Milsom when the ward doors opened and in walked the most strikingly good-looking woman Dido had ever seen. This tall, dark-haired beauty looked around coolly and then, spotting Dido, walked slowly up to her.

'Nurse, I'm looking for Dr James Dauntcey,' she said haughtily, her dark eyes barely registering Dido's presence.

'He's just finished his ward round. I could try his office if it's important,' Dido said with icy politeness.

'Yes. Could you do that?' The woman still gazed round the ward as if Dido had somehow hidden Dr Dauntcey and she was determined to find him.

Dido had a chance to study this extraordinary vision of chic, beauty and wealth. From the toes of her grey snakeskin shoes to the grey cashmere suit and cream silk blouse, to the top of her immaculately coiffed dark hair, she was stamped as rich, well-bred and stylish.

Dido was suddenly painfully aware of her unflattering nurse's uniform, her sensible, slightly worn shoes, her unsculpted hairstyle and her complete lack of make-up. She felt utterly outclassed by the tall, glamorous woman who stood impatiently beside her.

Dido picked up the telephone receiver. 'Who shall I say wants him?' she queried.

The woman turned her head to look Dido full in the face for the first time. Her eyes were deep-set and so dark that there seemed to be not one spark of light within them. 'Just say it's Lady Dauntcey,' she said precisely, and then looked away as if to dismiss Dido from her thoughts.

Dido was grateful that she was not still watching her, for the impact of that name made her reel and almost faint. She put a hand on the desk to steady herself, the blood was pounding in her ears. She felt only her grip on the cool receiver kept her from sinking to her knees with shock. Lady Dauntcey! Her worst fears had come true.

Slowly Dido dialled the extension number for Dr Dauntcey's office. Just as it began to ring, the ward doors banged and the tall figure of James Dauntcey came striding onto the ward.

'Staff!' he called to her, and then stopped in his tracks as he noticed the woman who stood beside Dido. His face broke into a delighted smile. 'Olivia!' he murmured, 'what a lovely surprise,' and in two strides he was embracing her, quite oblivious of Dido who stood ashen-faced, her hands so tightly clasped it seemed she was trying to keep herself from falling apart.

'Come, let's go and have a coffee.' With that, Dr Dauntcey put his arm round Lady Dauntcey's beauti-fully clad shoulders and steered her towards the doors. Just as he was about to close the ward door behind them, he looked back at Dido. 'Staff, I'm sorry I forgot. I came back for my stethoscope. Could you put it on one side for me? I'll pop in later and collect it.' And together the impressive and handsome pair walked down the corridor towards his office.

How well suited they are, Dido thought numbly as she gazed after their retreating backviews. How could she have ever thought he'd love her? How naive of her not to realise that the great Dr Dauntcey was bound to be married, and married to someone as imperious and nobly good-looking as himself.

Dido's knees were weak and a tremendous fatigue threatened to overwhelm her. She sank into her chair, her eyes downcast so that none of her patients could see her stricken face. She longed to bury her head in her outstretched arms and sob her heart out, it was so fit to burst. But she was a nurse first and foremost and the welfare of her patients was her responsibility. Somehow she would have to get through the day, on will-power alone if necessary.

Dido stood up, smoothed down her uniform and set off up the right side of the ward to start the morning's monitoring of pulses, blood pressures and temperatures. She could not allow herself to think of anything other than the job in hand. She could not risk facing her grief, not yet.

As she leaned over Mr Jameson, tragically still in coma after his sub-arachnoid haemorrhage and now with very little hope of recovery, Dido felt ashamed of her own unhappiness. She had health and youth, she had no business being miserable, she told herself sternly. But reason and common sense could not shift the physical aching in her chest, the terrible emptiness and sense of loss and betrayal.

Suddenly there was a hand on her arm and Dido turned to see Frank Berenson's warm, kindly face. His smile immediately turned to an expression of alarm.

'Di, are you all right? You look dreadful.'

Dido managed a tremulous smile. 'I'm OK, thanks, Frank.' She quickly turned her eyes from his face, for she found it hard to pretend.

'You're not OK. Even I can see that! You've been overdoing it. Look, why don't you come to the Founder's Day concert tonight? Everybody's going. It should be good music and some fun. Do come, Di, it would do you good. Get out and enjoy yourself a bit.'

Dido hesitated. Her first reaction was to get home as quickly as possible, crawl into bed and hide her grief in sleep. But the more realistic prospect of a desperate, sleepless night held out little attraction. Frank, too, was so gentle and concerned, so keen to take her out and treat her.

'Yes. That would be lovely, Frank. Thanks,' she said as enthusiastically as she could.

'Great! Then I'll pick you up about seven. That'll give you enough time to change. See you then.' He walked off with a bounce in his step.

Dido nodded and then quickly looked away as tears sprang inadvertently into her eyes. How cruel it was that she could not love in return the good man who loved her, and yet the man to whom she had given her heart was barely aware of the gift. And unwilling and unable to give anything in return, Dido thought bleakly.

She resolutely blinked back the tears and continued on her round.

CHAPTER SEVEN

By THE time Dido's duty had ended, she was feeling so tired and unwell that the last thing she wanted to do was to go out for the evening. But she could not let Frank down. She walked home as fast as she could and entered the cold dark flat. Not even Millie would be there to liven things up, for she was working a late shift. Dido shivered and turned on the gas fire. As she lit it with a match she noticed her hand was trembling.

There was not much time to eat and change so Dido quickly heated up some quiche left over from the day before. She stripped off her uniform and hurriedly pulled on the first warm garment she found in her wardrobe, an amber wool dress which set off her eyes.

She was surprised at how cold and shivery she felt. Perhaps she was succumbing to a bout of flu, she wondered as she pulled a brush through her hair. It was so easy for doctors and nurses to become hypochondriacs, imagining every headache to be a brain tumour and every sniffle to be flu, but Dido thought on this occasion she was not exaggerating her symptoms. A small anti-flu cocktail would do her no harm. She just had time to make her home-made concoction of two soluble aspirin, half a teaspoon of vitamin C powder and some nutmeg and honey in half a cup of hot water.

Suddenly there was the shrill ring of the doorbell. Dido gulped down the mixture, grabbed her coat and bag and ran down the stairs to open the door to Frank.

'You look a bit better already,' he said, peering

129

closely at her. 'But you just wait, a dose of Elgar will have you back to your effervescent self again.'

He led her to his Alfa Romeo and Dido climbed into the small, warm interior. She sighed and relaxed. It was such a luxury to travel by car on a cold night when you were not particularly well. Most of the time Dido did not mind going everywhere by public transport, or on foot, but when it was cold or late, or she was very tired, she longed to be able to jump into a little reliable car and motor home.

The concert hall was part of a new arts centre built in the City, only ten minutes' ride from the hospital. That evening there was to be a special performance of music to mark St Benedict's Founder's Day and as Dido and Frank walked in through the main doors and joined the throng at the bar, they greeted many familiar faces.

Frank thrust himself through the crush and eventually returned with a gin and tonic for Dido and a whisky for himself. He was smiling.

'I was just thinking about poor Mr Manetti and our reading him the riot act on the dangers of drink!' He handed Dido her glass and drank from his own. 'Mm, I needed that. I suppose that's when it gets dangerous—when on really *needs* a drink in order to feel human again. When I'm really tired and come off duty, I must admit a glass of whisky holds out enormous attractions.'

Dido nodded. 'I know, I'm only drinking this because I feel in need of a pick-me-up and I'm hoping the gin will do the trick. But it's probably a false sense of well-being.'

Frank was pressed against Dido by the crowds. Gazing down on her, he swallowed and said, rather self-consciously, 'Di, I know it's nothing to do with me, and you can bite my head off if you like, but,' and he paused and swallowed again, 'I've noticed how fond you've been getting of James Dauntcey. Do be careful. I'd hate to see you hurt.' His expression was a mixture of earnestness and embarrassment and he looked away, unwilling to witness the pain in Dido's face.

The last thing she needed was to be reminded of what a fool she had been, of how raw her emotions still were. She could not trust herself to speak and just nodded and then gulped a mouthful of her drink.

'It's only because I care for you so much that I'd ever dream of saying anything. You know that, don't you?'

Dido had got her emotions under control and she felt a wave of gratitude for Frank's enduring affection.

'Thank you for being so concerned. There's nothing between Dr Dauntcey and me. I may have had a crush on him at first, but I know better now.'

She had spoken in calm, measured tones but her whole being seemed to cry out, *No! it's not true! it's a once-in-a-lifetime passion that will last until I die! I'll never be able to feel this way for anyone else* . . .

Dido involuntarily put her hand to her throat to stop herself uttering those fateful words. How doomed she felt at the prospect of loving for ever someone who could not return that love.

Frank was talking about another interesting case on Hartland ward but, for once, Dido was incapable of conjuring up a show of interest in the clinical details. With a sense of relief, she noticed that the crush of people was thinning out as the audience made its way to their seats. The concert hall was modern and rather grand, the stalls sweeping round in a semi-circle, lit overhead by enormous steel and glass chandeliers which glittered like constellations of stars in the lofty auditorium. Frank had bought the best seats, in the centre front of the stalls, and he and Dido took their places amongst the glamorously attired concert-goers.

The lights dimmed and an expectant hush descended on the audience. The conductor raised his baton to begin. The London Symphony Orchestra were to perform Elgar's *Enigma Variations* and as the conductor's hand fell the hall was suddenly filled with celestial music. Dido leaned back in her comfortable seat and closed her eyes. The waves of sound washed up from the orchestra podium, just a few yards away, and healed her battered spirits.

Dido's tensions melted away, her mind roamed freely wherever the music prompted. Suddenly there was the image of her music mistress at school, who had been a great Elgar enthusiast. Dido remembered a particular term when every music lesson had started with one of the variations. Their mistress would then explain that each was a musical portrait of the composer's friends and relatives. Dido could see her still, standing in front of the class, her eyes half closed as she listened to Elgar's most famous work.

Dido sat, eyes half-closed too, and the music seemed to lift her out of her pain. She still felt tired, but the hard lump of bitterness and despair had dissolved and trickled away. For the first time in days, Dido felt free of tension and anxiety.

Suddenly the interval had arrived and a burst of clapping and cheering accompanied the musicians' departure backstage. Dido and Frank remained in their seats rather than fight their way to the bar. Instead, they discussed the performance and surveyed the audience, enjoying spotting familiar faces from the hospital. Dido was sorry Millie had been working late, for she would have enjoyed the evening tremendously. She caught sight of Millie's boss sitting next to a good-looking blonde woman who appeared to be a good twenty years younger than he was.

'Look, Frank, there's Mr de Vere Thomas. Do you suppose that lady is his wife?' Dido whispered with a wicked smile.

'Most unlikely,' Frank said, narrowing his eyes to get a better look.

A little of Dido's old buoyancy had returned as she sat back again. Then a movement caught her eye. A man and a woman were returning to their seats just a little to the left of her and a couple of rows in front. From a distance they both looked familiar and as they approached her heart began to beat at a sickening speed.

Lady Dauntcey, dressed dazzlingly in a cream satin suit, led the way. But the sight that set off every alarm and pain system in Dido's body was the tall dark man who followed her. His head was bent and slightly turned from her but the darkness, the profile, the general impressive stature and mien were unmistakable. Dr James Dauntcey was spending the evening at a concert with his beautiful wife. And as Dido's eyes followed the dark line of his suit she saw his fine hand intertwined with hers.

The pain and jealousy that engulfed her shocked Dido with its intensity. She looked away, her face white and her eyes blank with misery. Then, irresistibly, her gaze was drawn back again to the couple just about to take their seats. As if he somehow felt the burning laser of her eyes on him, the man turned and looked Dido full in the face.

James, James, acknowledge me, smile, incline your head, anything. Just don't deny my existence! she begged him silently. But his handsome face remained strange and expressionless, as if he seemed to see yet not recognise her. Then his wife took his hand and pulled him gently into the seat beside her.

The conductor had returned and the lights once more dimmed. The aching beauty of the music seemed not to soothe but to echo and enhance the ache in Dido's heart. She did not know how she could sit through another hour without collapsing under the strain of keeping her emotions in check. Frank, sensing something was wrong, took her hand gently in his and held it tight, as if he was her lifeline and she set adrift in a turbulent sea.

At last the thunder of applause died away and Dido was free to go. She felt as if she was released from an emotional bondage worse than any prison. Ducking her head so as not to see, or be seen, by Dr Dauntcey, she followed Frank to the exit.

'Are you all right? You look like death warmed up,' he asked her with real concern.

She nodded. 'I'm just not feeling very well. It's probably flu or something. I'll take two aspirin when I go to bed.'

They had just emerged into the cold dark night. Dido made to cross the road to walk the short distance to the car when she was pulled sharply back to the pavement by Frank. A gleaming white Mercedes swished across their path and came to a halt at the concert hall's entrance.

'Don't forget to look where you're going,' Frank said protectively, and as they walked round the bonnet of the huge car Dido looked back over her shoulder. Two distinguished-looking people stood in the blazing light of the entrance long enough for her to recognise Lady Dauntcey, swathed now in a full-length white mink, and James Dauntcey beside her in a long black overcoat with a luxurious Persian lamb collar. How beautiful they looked. Dido watched as he led the way to the Mercedes, whose door was held open by its chauffeur, and the glamorous couple settled into the red leather interior and were driven off at speed.

Curious as to what had attracted Dido's attention, Frank too turned to look.

'Phew, what a car!' he said appreciatively. Then he looked again as the car passed, 'That chap in the back looks remarkably like our own Dr D,' he said with surprise.

'That's because he is,' Dido said in a small, cracked voice.

'Are you sure, Di? I left the hospital late and the noble doctor was still slaving away on some tricky diagnosis. He must be a veritable superman to make it to the concert—and all togged up in such glad rags!'

But Dido was too physically exhausted and emotionally drained to entertain any speculations. She was grateful for Frank's arm round her shoulders, for his grip kept her upright and able to walk.

'Di, you shouldn't come into work tomorrow. I really think you need some time off to get better. Do stop driving yourself so hard.' They were sitting in the car outside Dido's flat and Frank looked as concerned as she looked deathly pale. 'Shall I take your temperature and blood pressure?' he said, leaning over into the back to get his case.

'Don't worry, Frank. I won't come in tomorrow if I'm still feeling so lousy. I promise. I think some aspirin and a good night's sleep might make all the difference.' Then she managed an appreciative smile and leaned over quickly and kissed him on the cheek. 'Thanks very much for a lovely concert. The music was super. I'm just sorry I wasn't better company.' Before he could open the door for her, Dido had climbed out of the car and walked up to the flat's front door.

She could barely summon the energy to undress and wash, and the moment she put her head on the pillow sleep claimed her exhausted body.

The next morning Dido awoke feeling better, but still very tired. Tiredness could become a constant companion of nurses and Dido would have felt a fraud using that as a reason for not going to work.

She arrived on the ward to find that Staff Nurse Anne Bradshaw had had a frantically busy night duty with two more emergency admissions.

'Di, I couldn't be more pleased to hand this lot over to you. I'm dead beat!' Anne greeted her, looking slightly distraught. 'Frank's been marvellous. He's been here most of the night, poor man.'

Dido thought of Frank, returning home from the concert, looking forward to bed, and then called in by the hospital to spend the rest of the night dealing with emergencies. Her own fatigue seemed to diminish in the face of that. She took off her coat and prepared to start the day.

'Okay. Tell me the worst,' she said, walking back to Anne's side. She was still sitting at the desk, filling in the Kardex.

'Well, we lost one last night, I'm afraid. Mr Jameson, with the sub-arachnoid haemorrhage. He never regained consciousness, as you know. Then last night he must have bled again. His blood pressure went up and pulse rate down. Cheyne-Stokes respiration warned us he was fading fast. The periods when he wasn't breathing got more and more protracted. He died at about two o'clock this morning.'

Dido knew that those were the bare facts of a case that

had a tragic domestic side. His death had widowed his young wife and made four little children fatherless. The first haemorrhage had struck him down swiftly and without warning, and as he continued in deep coma hopes for his recovery had grown increasingly slender. Dido rationalised that, in a way, his death was the only way out of an impossible situation.

She shook her head sadly. 'I suppose you've contacted his wife?'

'Yes. She's been in most of each day, as you know. She took it very calmly. I think these last days have prepared her for the fact that her husband was unlikely to recover.'

'And on top of Mr Jameson's death, you had emergency admissions as well. No wonder you were busy.'

'You could say that!' Anne expostulated. 'A Mr Brian James with hypo-mania. His wife couldn't cope with him any more and he came in in the company of four large ambulance men. He was in one of those manic expansive moods, insisting he's all right, offering to write the hospital a cheque for a million pounds, chatting up the nurses and talking nineteen to the dozen. He was quite a handful, I can tell you!'

Dido smiled, imagining how he must have livened up the ward. 'I suppose he was exhibiting the typical lack of inhibition and boundless energy?' she enquired.

'That's an understatement! No nurse was safe in his immediate vicinity. His wife said he hasn't slept for a week. He's been writing reams and reams of something he calls *The Greatest Story Ever Told*, probably a fantastical autobiography.'

'Oh dear, poor chap. Then the other side of that mood swing is deepest depression that can descend without warning and stay for weeks. I suppose you had to sedate him?' Dido followed Anne's eyes to where, at the far side of the ward, a middle-aged man sat, reading the newspaper with apparently perfect decorum.

'Yes. Haloperidol intra-muscularly, and he's back on Lithium. Apparently he'd been prescribed it before but had stopped taking it on a whim.'

'So I suppose we'll be waiting for a psychiatric opinion. No special nursing necessary?' Dido looked questioningly at Anne Bradshaw.

'No, he's still a bit unstable, so keep your eye on him. It's a pity he's in a bed rather far from your desk.'

Dido's extreme tiredness had returned and she was grateful for the seat Anne had just vacated. She had begun to realise that there might be something more seriously wrong with her. A little trickle of fear slipped into her consciousness, but before she had time to speculate further along the lines of leukaemia, kidney failure or muscular dystrophy, Anne interrupted her thoughts.

'The second new admission was Mr Toby Smythe, in the bed by the door. Acute asthma attack. He came in straight from work, where he'd had a blazing row with his boss, and apparently practically died in Casualty. They gave him oxygen and then Aminophylline and corticosteroids intravenously.'

'He looks all right now,' Dido said, noticing the good colour in the cheeks of the young man who sat in the chair by his bed.

'Yes. Thank goodness! You should have seen him last night, fighting for his breath—and his life. I think an acute asthma attack must be as frightening to watch as it is to suffer.' She looked down at the Kardex. 'He's on oral steroids now.'

Dido nodded. 'I suppose he had a chest X-ray on the way up to the ward?'

'Mm. They were afraid of a coincidental pneumothorax, but luckily all they could find was the typically over-inflated lungs. We were doing blood gases hourly and a peak expiratory flow rate to find out how tight his lungs were.'

'And our old patients? Have they all been progressing to plan?' Dido hoped there had been no setbacks and unforseen complications.

'Luckily, yes. Mr Milsom's endocarditis is clearing up as expected. It's a long job though, I think he'll be here for another five weeks or more.' Staff Nurse Bradshaw quickly outlined the conditions of the other patients, for she had been due to go off duty half an hour previously and she was more than ready for her bed.

Dido bid her goodbye. She called her nurses and asked them to straighten up the beds and draw the curtains ready for the consultant's round. Once more the puzzle of her own symptoms intruded into her brain. She was now feeling quite distinctly shivery and if there had been time would have taken her temperature. If Frank could spare a moment after the round she thought she would ask his advice.

All too soon the ward doors swung open and a trio of grim-looking doctors entered. Frank looked exhausted, with great blue semi-circles under his eyes. Russell seemed uncharacteristically gloomy and Dr Dauntcey looked positively thunderous.

'Right,' he grunted, 'let's start immediately,' and he strode off to see Mr Milsom, followed by his entourage of doctors and a couple of nurses. For a moment, Dido felt quite dizzy and nauseous and had to sit down on the chair by her desk to collect herself. Just as she was about to get up and join the round, she saw a stony-faced James Dauntcey stride over to her side.

'Staff, Mr Milsom should be getting out of bed for a walk for a few minutes each day. Make a note of that, would you?' Then he paused and looked accusingly at her. 'Where were you when I rang last night?'

Dido was so taken aback, so puzzled by the question, that she was sure her mouth must have dropped open. Her flummoxed brain could not find an appropriate answer but before she could say a word he had turned on his heel and walked back to his group, who had already moved on to the next patient.

Dido had taken it for granted that, after his wife's unexpected arrival on the ward, Dr Dauntcey was unlikely to ring her. And Dido herself would certainly have been unwilling to entertain any proposal that was not strictly professional. And anyway, her tired brain puzzled, *when* could he have rung? After all, he had been at the concert too—and in the company of his wife. Whatever it all meant, it was too much for Dido to fathom in her present unwell condition. All she knew was that he was mad at her for not being there when he rang!

Dido joined the group around Brian James' bed just in time to hear the end of Mr James' animated tirade.

'It's all a terrible mistake. I shouldn't be here at all, I've got so much important work to do on my *magnum opus*, you know. The publishers are clamouring for it, it'll make me a million. I *must* get home! It's all a mistake, my wife just got a little over-distraught, can't keep up with me. She hasn't much stamina, you know . . .'

'OK, Mr James,' Dr Dauntcey's deep voice interrupted the flow of words. 'You're right. We don't need to keep you here much longer, but you must get into the habit of taking the pills we prescribe you. They really do help balance your swings of mood so they're less extreme . . .'

These were the last words Dido heard, for a terrible pounding sound filled her head and a wave of heat overcame her. She was aware of the strength ebbing from her limbs as, uttering a small moan, she collapsed on the floor.

The first person to reach her side was Dr James Dauntcey, his face suddenly haggard with anxiety. In one swift movement he had scooped up Dido's limp body in his arms and, calling for the nurses, carried her through into the adjacent private ward.

There he lay her gently on the bed, loosened the crisp white collar of her dress and took her wrist to count her pulse. In that long minute, Dr Dauntcey gazed down at her beautiful face, made all the more haunting by its paleness. Her red-gold hair had somehow become freed from the knot she wore it in for work. Her exposed throat seemed so vulnerable and strangely intimate in its white-skinned slenderness.

'Nurse, please loosen Staff Nurse's clothes, I have to listen to her chest.' His words were crisp and to the point and, as the young nurse unbuttoned Dido's dress he left the room to pace outside.

Dido came round just as the nurse was pulling the sheet up over her shoulders. 'I didn't faint, did I?' she asked in an unsteady voice.

'Dr Dauntcey's just investigating what's wrong with you,' the young nurse said, then scurried out.

'Oh no,' Dido moaned under her breath and then looked up to see a grim-faced Dr Dauntcey re-enter the room.

'You gave us all a fright, Staff,' he said without a smile. 'Have you been feeling unwell?' His manner was so formal, Dido could hardly believe this was the same man who had held her hand and whispered her name with such longing.

'I've been feeling terribly tired and a little feverish these last two days,' she answered with an equally deadpan expression.

'Well, your pulse is normal. I just want to examine you.'

He was about to turn down the sheet to expose her chest, as he had done many thousands of times before with as many patients, but this time he hesitated. 'I can get a nurse in here if you'd like,' he said, averting his eyes and looking slightly disconcerted.

'No, it's all right,' Dido said quietly, and then, to save him embarrassment, she turned the sheet down herself to expose just enough of her breasts to enable him to listen to her chest.

Placing his two fingers flat on her ribs, he tapped them with the middle finger of his other hand, concentrating on listening to the resonance. All the while he avoided Dido's eyes.

She watched him, her own embarrassment having faded, and she noticed that his colour was heightened and his frown more deeply etched between his dark brows. Dido did not need to be told that the dull sound the tapping elicited meant her lungs were partially consolidated with fluid. And she knew that could mean pneumonia.

She watched Dr Dauntcey's frown spread across his brow. Without a word he put his stethoscope to her chest and listened to her heart sounds. Dido hoped to goodness they were normal. She felt weak and feverish and a little alarmed as to what disease or condition had struck her down so surprisingly.

'Would you sit up, Staff?' Dr Dauntcey's suddenly tender voice roused her from her thoughts. 'I just want to listen to your lungs.'

Holding the sheet to her breasts, for she was strangely shy of him, Dido sat up and leaned forward slightly so that he could put his stethoscope on her back. He sat on the bed beside her and placed the stethoscope against her skin. A violent shiver ran down her spine. Dido was not certain if it was the fever, the cold of the metal or the proximity of the doctor which produced such a tremulous sensation in her. She did not presume to think that the exposure of her white shoulders and the fleeting glimpse of her breasts might have had the same effect on him.

As he sat beside her, uneasily aware of the faint perfume of her skin, Dr Dauntcey tried not to notice the vulnerable curve of her slender back, the delicate junction of neck with shoulder, the swell of her breast.

'There are areas of consolidation, aren't there?' Dido turned her head to meet his gaze for the first time. Once again, those intensely blue eyes and hers of amber-gold were united involuntarily in a moment's recognition. Dido felt her heart leap, as if to shine from her eyes the message, *I love you*. But she abruptly turned her eyes away. How could she even *think* that emotion when she knew he was committed to another? She held the sheet tightly against her chest, her hands clenched till her knuckles grew white.

As if his words came to her muffled by distance, Dido heard his opinion of her condition. 'There's no point in keeping anything from you. Yes, there could be consolidation. This is very like old-style pneumonia, but there's another possibility.' He stood up and walked to the window.

'Well? You have to tell me, you know. Your patient is not unaware of the possibilities,' Dido said quietly as she lay down again, tired out, her mind racing with the text book reasons for inflammation of the lungs.

Dr Dauntcey turned from the window and smiled. 'I'm quite aware that I am dealing with an extraordinary patient.' He took a deep breath. 'The other possibility I'm afraid of is tuberculosis. I haven't forgotten your nursing Mr Manton so conscientiously before his condition was fully diagnosed. I'm going to order a sputum test and a chest X-ray and hope I'm wrong.'

Dido's spirits sank further. She had had that fear too, but had dismissed it. The prospect was daunting. Not only was the disease unpleasant and dangerous, but nasty complications were not unknown and the convalescent period would mean she was off work for at least a month or two.

She felt a light touch on her bare shoulder and looked up with a brave smile. 'Don't worry, little Dido. We'll look after you.' James Dauntcey's words were so softly spoken and the expression on his face so sweet and caring that Dido was transported away from fear and into a state of acceptance and trust. Her tiredness could no longer be denied and as she slipped into sleep she heard over and over again those softly spoken words.

Dido awoke to the clattering of a portable X-ray machine. As she struggled to sit up she thought how strange it was to be on the other side of the fence, a patient, ministered to by one's colleagues and suffering all the helplessness and indignities that illness thrust upon one. She sat there as the radiographers slipped the cold plate behind her back, cracking jokes to which she barely had the energy to respond. Dido felt she was only just up to holding her breath when requested, as they exposed the film.

As the heavy X-ray machine was manoeuvred awkwardly out of the door again, Dido saw Millie's cheerful face pop up behind the glass door. She thought what a welcome sight she was.

'Di, I've just heard about you passing out. What on earth's wrong?' Millie sat on the chair beside her bed and gazed at Dido with concern.

'Oh, goodness knows. There's some consolidation in my lungs, my temperature's up a bit, I feel chronically tired. I suppose pneumonia—or there's an outside chance it's TB.'

Millie gasped. 'No! It can't be! Where could you have picked that up?'

Dido sighed and said in a resigned tone of voice, 'I was nursing, and aspirating, a patient with undiagnosed TB. I suppose it could have been that, although these days it's not considered to be so very infectious. But let's not expect the worst.' Her voice trailed off. She was so very weary now.

'I can see you're exhausted. One piece of news to cheer you. I'll be nursing you. I asked Matron if I could be transferred to your ward—now you're ill they're in need of a staff nurse and my ward is over-staffed. So here I am. But I'll warn you, there'll be no sloppy behaviour or malingering.' Millie stood to attention with a business-like expression on her face, then smiled and winked. 'Miss Alexander, I'm ordering you to take a good nap now, while you can. You just wait till we start treatment—it'll be all go!' And Millie left the side ward and quietly closed the door.

She was much more concerned about her friend's condition than she had let on. Dido's pallor and her symptoms came as a shock to Millie. She felt suddenly guilty that she had not realised earlier that Dido was so unwell. Small incidents over the previous few days immediately sprang to her mind, hindsight now adding significance to those episodes of tiredness and depression.

Millie was pleased to be taking on Dido's job for her, particularly as it meant she would be responsible for the day nursing of Dido herself. As she walked towards Millington ward, she heard hurrying footsteps along the corridor behind her. Turning her head quickly, she was surprised to see an exceptionally handsome dark man pass her and push his way through the ward doors. His distinguished suit and confident air meant he was probably one of the consultants, and Millie suddenly smiled to herself as she realised which consultant he was most likely to be.

She had only seen Dr James Dauntcey a couple of times before, both in conditions of dimness or distance. The party had been the first time, and the second he had paused in the corridor to talk to Frank but had disappeared by the time Millie had approached and curiously asked Frank who he was. This handsome, hurrying man had to be the same one, Millie thought as she followed him into the ward.

Millie looked around curiously. Dr Dauntcey was nowhere to be found. Then she noticed that the door to the side ward, where Dido lay, was ajar. Thinking she may be needed for some medical procedure, Millie walked up to the door, but something made her pause at the threshold.

She looked into the small bare room. The blind was

drawn and a hazy light filtered onto the neatly-made bed where her friend lay. Dido's mass of hair streamed out over the pillows, creating a striking frame for her translucently pale skin. But more striking by far was the surprising presence of Dr Dauntcey in the room. He sat on the bed with his back to the door. Millie could see his face in profile as he gazed on the sleeping Dido. He cradled one of her slender hands in both of his. Surely he can't be taking her pulse? Millie thought to herself.

Then Millie looked down at Dido and saw what Dr Dauntcey undoubtedly saw. Her heart-shaped face, suddenly seeming so fragile, the fine eyebrows arching over lids closed and tinged with mauve. Perhaps he was counting her respiration, she thought, for even from the doorway Millie could tell it was rapid and shallow, her breath emitted with a slight hiss from between pale lips.

Millie knew she ought to advertise her presence and not watch unseen, but some instinct made her loath to interrupt the intimate scene in the room. Even in profile, Dr Dauntcey's face displayed his anguish. Deep lines were etched into his cheeks. His hooded eyes did not leave Dido's face for an instant and he leaned over her with such intensity, as if wishing to communicate something of his will to her.

Millie knew she was witnessing some private emotion, yet she could not fathom exactly what it meant. She felt it better if she tiptoed away. She entered the main ward just in time to see Mr James, the hypo-manic patient she had been warned about, disappear out of the main ward doors.

Millie quickly caught up with him. 'Where are you going, Mr James?' she asked him, firmly taking his arm.

'Home. I've got important things to do. You medical drones don't understand the responsibilities of a genius.

I've got volumes that need to be written, life sciences waiting to be discovered. I can't hang about here until some crackpot doctor deigns to turn up and see me!'

Millie knew it would be impossible to impress upon him, while he was in one of his manic moods, that he was ill and needed help. She also knew she was not strong enough to restrain him.

In a panic she thought of how Dido would tackle the problem of getting this patient to return peaceably and happily to bed. Inspiration struck. She would meet his grandiose view of the world and his place in it with her own equally inflated version.

'Mr James, I've got some very exciting news for you. Because you are so important and interesting, the world-famous Dr Burnie is flying in specially to see you. He wants to write up your biography for his latest book! So come back to bed now and get ready for his arrival.'

Mr James turned to face Millie, his intention to leave arrested by the thought that his genius would be recognised at last. He courteously took Millie's arm and allowed himself to be escorted back to bed as if he was Cinderella going to the ball. Millie did not feel too troubled by her exaggeration of the truth. After all, Dr Burnie was very well thought of and Mr James's case might well get into print in one of the learned psychiatric journals.

Just as she had finished settling Mr James, Millie glanced up to see Dr Dauntcey enter the main ward again. Unaware of her scrutiny, his face seemed haggard and deeply troubled. Millie walked up to him.

'Good morning, sir. I'm Staff Nurse Millie Simpson. I've taken over the ward for the time being.'

'Good morning, Staff,' he said distractedly. 'I'm worried about Staff Nurse Alexander. Are you a friend of hers?' He looked up and met her gaze. Millie was surprised by the blue of his eyes and the intensity of their expression, the intimation of pain and passion in their depths. Trust Dido to fall for an ice and fire merchant like this one, she thought to herself.

'Yes, she's my flatmate,' Millie said, deciding against adding that she was also her best friend.

'Well the lab has come back with a preliminary finding on the sputum test which makes me certain that she's got TB.'

'Oh no,' Millie said softly, under her breath.

'I'm going to start treatment without delay. Any changes at all in respiration or blood pressure must be reported directly to me or my registrar.' He strode off, then turned abruptly. 'Oh, and for goodness' sake wear a gown and mask when nursing her. I don't want any more cases on the ward!'

'Well!' Millie thought to herself. 'Poor Di!' She was not just thinking about her illness. That man is trouble, she thought grimly, wishing her best friend had never clapped eyes on him. Not only was he haughty and imperious, he was so good-looking and eligible he would be bound to have several wives, or mistresses at least, tucked away in his private life.

Still musing over the problem, Millie put on a disposable mask and a newly-laundered gown and walked over to Dido's room. She opened the door quietly and was relieved to see Dido turn her head and manage a weak smile.

'Is that you, Millie, behind all that camouflage?' she asked in a whisper.

'It sure is, Di,' Millie said as she walked up to her bedside.

'All this gown and mask business means I've got the

dreaded TB, I suppose.' Dido looked sad and wan as she gazed wide-eyed up at her friend.

It was not a question, so Millie did not answer directly but sat beside her and took her hand. 'How're you feeling, love?'

'Pretty lousy. I suppose you'll start filling me up with drugs soon?'

'Yes. The devilishly good-looking Dr Dauntcey has just buzzed off but he'll be back to OK the doses. Any minute I've got to start sticking needles into you.'

Dido smiled, 'Do you think he's good-looking?' she asked curiously.

'Yes, dangerously so. So don't go getting any ideas. Remember our pact. No doctor-nurse romancing for us. It's very bad for the heart!'

CHAPTER EIGHT

DIDO LAY in her narrow hospital bed and gazed at the bare pastel walls. A dull cloud of depression settled over her. It was not that she feared tuberculosis, although the name of the disease had always been synonomous with a slow and inevitable death. She was well aware how successful the treatment was these days, especially when diagnosed early. But she also knew it was a long drawn out thing, that she would feel dreadful for days and be off work for weeks longer. As a nurse, she felt she had committed the ultimate folly—she had fallen ill herself. Dido thought bleakly that her rating with Dr Dauntcey must have slipped to zero, if it had not been that low already.

Not that any of that fantasy mattered any more, she hurriedly reminded herself. After all, he was doubly unsuitable. He was a consultant and he was married. As Millie would be quick to point out, he was a staggeringly unsuitable object for her passion. Sighing, Dido passed a hand across her damp brow. She was feverish and had developed an irritating, non-productive cough. She wondered what her X-ray would show.

The door opened quietly and Dido turned her head, gasping in amazement at the sight which greeted her. Millie staggered into the room carrying an enormous bouquet of white roses and cream madonna lilies.

'Somebody must love you, Di,' Millie said, laying the beautiful flowers gently on the table at the foot of her bed.

'Who're they from?' Dido asked her weakly.

'I thought you'd know. There's no card, they just arrived this morning. That posh florist, Westbrook, brought them.'

'I have absolutely no idea.' Dido was puzzled. Her parents were still on holiday in Tunisia and, anyway, would never have sent such an extravagant bunch.

'Well, they're beautiful. And the smell!' Millie wrinkled up her small nose appreciatively and started to arrange the flowers in two vases she had brought from the sluice room. Dido watched her friend and realised just how the mask she had to wear obscured so much of her face and expression. It also made her, the patient, feel separate and isolated.

Millie had finished her arrangements and walked over to the bedside. Dido could tell by the crinkling of her eyes that she was smiling.

'Your X-ray is due back any minute and I have orders to get Frank and Dr Dauntcey up to see it. They'll probably let you have a look, too.'

Dido closed her eyes and dozed off as her friend took her wrist and counted her pulse. Then Millie rolled up the loose sleeve of Dido's hospital gown, wrapped the cuff of the sphygmomanometer around her upper arm and pumped air into it.

Dido turned her head to watch as the mercury level rose and fell. She was a good enough patient to know not to talk while Millie was making her readings. But the moment she had finished writing them on the chart at the foot of her bed, Dido asked, 'Do me a favour, Millie? Could you ring my parents tomorrow? I think they get back from holiday tonight, but I'd like them to have a good night's sleep. Please tell them not to worry, that it's not serious and I'm in excellent hands.'

Just at that moment the door opened and two gowned
and masked male figures entered the room. Dido was
feeling extraordinarily weak and weepy. She longed to
be gathered up in strong male arms, to be loved and
protected and cared for. And although she would
not admit it, she longed for those arms to be James
Dauntcey's.

She met his eyes, all the more mesmerising as they
looked at her over the stark white of his mask. Did she
read concern and affection there, or was it merely her
wishful thinking?

His gaze did not falter as he said, waving at the
profusion of flowers, 'You must have an admirer, Miss
Alexander.'

Dido could only nod. She felt so hot and dry-throated
she could not trust her voice to utter anything more than
a croak.

'Hello, Di.' Frank moved closer. 'I'm very sorry to see
you like this. But you're in the best medical hands, as
you know. We'll get you up and off home in a week or so,
won't we, sir?' Frank looked back at Dr Dauntcey,
whose eyes had not left Dido's face.

Millie, too, had been watching Dido closely. Her
pallor, with only a hectic spot of red on each cheek,
made her seem ethereal and other-worldly. She was
drowsy too. It was Millie's job to watch her closely for
any signs of deterioration or complications, and she
intended to be conscientous to a fault.

Dr Dauntcey turned abruptly to Millie and said,
'Staff, chivvy up X-ray. I'd like to see Miss Alexander's
film before I go over to Hartland ward.' He walked to
Dido's side and sat on the chair by her bed. Such
proximity was almost unbearable for Dido in her
weakened state. She found it nearly impossible to

restrain the tears of bitterness and self-pity. Her
eyes seemed even larger and more shining in her pale
face as they rested fleetingly on Dr Dauntcey's face.

He took her hand in his and the intense expression
in his eyes softened with an emotion Dido did not
recognise.

'How are you feeling? Are you still coughing occasionally, or has it become more troublesome?' he
asked in the gentlest of voices.

Dido shook her head. 'It's about the same.' And then
the unshed tears almost spilled into her eyes as she felt
him softly lay his hand on her forehead.

'You're still feverish, aren't you?' he said. Then,
keeping his cool hand on her brow, he turned to Frank.
'What's the latest temperature reading on the chart?'

Frank scanned the chart and then looked up. 'One
hundred and two.'

'Mm.' James Dauntcey brought his hand down Dido's
cheek to lightly palpate the glands under her jaw. 'Mm,'
he said again, uncommunicatively. 'Staff, I want to
check her lymph nodes,' he called over his shoulder to
Millie, who had re-entered the room.

Millie stepped forward to undo the few buttons on the
front of Dido's gown and then stepped back nearer
Frank.

Dr Dauntcey's eyes were smiling as he said to Dido, 'I
hope my hands are warm enough.' Then he slipped
one hand into her armpit to gently palpate the gland
there.

Despite her weakness and fever, or perhaps partly
because of it, Dido was consumed with a longing for his
cool fingers to run the full length of her feverish body.
The desire was so strong in her that Dido felt sure
everyone in the room must be aware of an electrical

disturbance in the air. But no, Millie and Frank were exchanging a word or two at the foot of her bed and Dr Dauntcey, finishing his examination, had pulled the sheet up to her chin.

'They seem slightly enlarged. We'll have to watch that, Staff. Now where's this X-ray?' he said as he got up from the chair by Dido's bed.

'Here.' Millie held out the buff envelope.

'Good,' Dr Dauntcey said as he slipped the black film under the clips on the light box on the wall. He snapped on the fluorescent bulb that dispersed the light evenly through the sheet of milky glass. Dido craned her head to see and could just make out the two dark shapes of her lungs. Frank, Dr Dauntcey and Millie were peering at it closely. They muttered a few words to each other and then Frank switched off the light.

'Good,' Dr Dauntcey said, almost to himself. He walked back to Dido's bedside. 'There's a patch of pneumonia. No miliary deposits, which I'm delighted about, but with the sputum test results I'm afraid it's definitely TB.' He paused and his eyes narrowed as he watched her face for signs of any adverse reaction to the news. 'As you know, drug therapy has improved radically over the last decade or so. I'm aiming to have you on your feet in a week or less, although treatment will continue for at least six months.'

Dido nodded, almost too tired to speak.

'Now, get some sleep. I don't want any more alarms over your health.' His peremptory tone made her feel as if he was a stern but fond father chiding his daughter. In Dido's currently dependant state, such paternalism was not unwelcome.

They all left the room and Dido closed her eyes. The sweet, exotic smell of lilies filled her nostrils and she felt herself drifting off into a kind of half-sleep. Strange dreams beckoned, fragments of her conscious and unconscious life jostled in one vast panorama. She knew that she was in that uneasy state between a feverish wakefulness and proper deep sleep. She had no control over the images which filled her brain but she was somehow separate from them, watching. Dido grew increasingly tired and longed for the oblivion of real sleep, but it would not come.

Millie came to see her a couple of times to give her an injection and to record her body's rhythms, but Dido could not rouse herself from this twilight zone of semi-sleep. Her restless body seemed to toss and turn for hours, or was it only minutes? Dido had lost all sense of time and had not the energy or will to surface from sleep and look at her watch.

Then suddenly a great shaking fit woke her and she sat up in bed in fright. Her gown and the sheets were soaked in sweat and, to her greater alarm, everything she looked at appeared in double vision. It was dark outside. Dido had no idea of the time or what was happening to her. She put her finger on the bell by her bed and within the minute the night Staff Nurse, Julie Williams, was by her side.

'Hello, Di, what's wrong?' Two images of Julie's anxious face peered at her.

'For some reason I'm seeing double.' Dido's voice seemed to her to issue from some far-away place.

'You're also drenched in sweat. Let me take your temperature.' Dido opened her mouth and slipped the cold mercury bulb under her tongue. The double vision worried her because she knew it was a sign of meningitis, inflammation of the membranes around the brain, and a common companion of TB.

Julie Williams had left the room, probably to ring
Frank, Dido thought despondently, wishing she could
see and feel normally again. Just as the thermometer was
beginning to hurt the sensitive area under her tongue,
Julie returned, removed it and looked at the reading.
'One hundred and three, not too bad, considering,' she
said, half to herself.

The door to Dido's room opened again and Frank
Berenson walked in, looking tired and crumpled as he
hurriedly donned his mask. 'What's up, Di?' he said in a
voice that attempted to sound cheerful.

'I'm seeing double, Frank,' she said, looking up at
him, her face pale and cheeks coloured a hectic red.

'Are you also rather drowsy?' he said, taking her
hand.

'Well, I feel peculiar. Feverish, not quite in touch with
reality. I don't feel sleepy, but terribly tired.' Her voice
was faint and slightly shaky.

'I think a lumbar puncture's in order, Di. I want to
rule out tuberculous meningitis.'

Dido sighed and looked away. She felt so weak and on
the verge of tears that even the prospect of a lumbar
puncture, a relatively painless procedure, seemed to be
too much to bear.

She lay on her left side, her hospital gown pulled up
round her waist so that Frank had an unimpeded area of
back to work on. Staff Nurse Williams hurried off to set
up the trolley and Frank rolled up his sleeves and
scrubbed his hands and forearms thoroughly.

'You've got nothing to worry about, Di. I'm an expert
puncture man. I've practised on thousands in order to do
yours perfectly.' He was meaning to be jolly and reassuring but Dido could barely summon a smile. She knew it
was ridiculous to feel so sorry for herself but she had not

the energy to resist. She heard the rattle of the trolley as Julie wheeled it into the room, and then saw Frank walk over to take his place on the chair behind her.

'You know the procedure, Di. I'll swab your back— that might feel a bit cold—then the prick of the local anaesthetic. From then on you shouldn't feel a thing.'

Dido closed her eyes and a trickle of a tear rolled down her nose and onto the pillow. She heard the door behind her open softly and then close, a few quiet words spoken by Frank, but she could not catch them, so distant did everything but her own sensations seem.

Dido's eyes were still closed when she was aware of a prickle and then a sharp sting as the local anaesthetic went into her back. Just as another tear welled and trickled down her cheek, she felt her hand taken gently and squeezed. With a great effort of will, Dido managed to open her eyes. Inexplicably they seemed to have become as heavy as lead. Through the shimmer of her tears she saw Dr Dauntcey looking down at her, her hand cradled in his.

To Dido's befuddled brain, the expression in his face and the warmth and caring that shone from his eyes meant just one thing. He loved her. She was too weak and drowsy to question her assumption, or to discount its validity. She simply accepted the idea, that the man she loved loved her, without the slightest consideration of the past or concern for the future. And hugging that thrilling realisation to her heart, she closed her eyes again and drifted off into half-sleep.

Dr Dauntcey had been about to leave the hospital for home when he had been drawn to take one last look at Dido. He told himself it was purely concern for a fellow member of staff's health. But as he approached her room, he noticed the light was on and his heart gave a sickening lurch. What could be wrong? What drama was being played out in that small room? His footsteps quickened and his brain started to race with lurid possibilities. When he finally opened the door to see Frank performing nothing more alarming than a lumbar puncture, his fears were partially allayed.

He watched for a moment as Frank withdrew the needle and a bright drop of blood sprang out of the perfect, moon-white curve of her exposed back.

'Staff, tell the lab I want the results on that CSF through as quickly as possible. It should only take an hour, so I'll wait. I'd like to know if she's clear or not.'

Julie Williams nodded. She thought how extremely conscientious it was of him to wait. He could have left it to Frank just as easily. But then Dr Dauntcey had won himself a reputation as a meticulous and dedicated doctor who had not allowed his status to remove him from the everyday care of his patients.

Frank had wished them goodnight and Staff Julie Williams had wheeled away the trolley. Dr Dauntcey sat down in the dimly-lit room and pulled a book of Shelley's poems from his pocket. He started to read.

Dido emerged slightly from her feverish sleep. She sensed someone else was in the room but she could not see properly, curled as she was on her side with her back to the door. With a sigh, she rolled onto her back. She turned her head and could not quite believe her eyes. She must be hallucinating now, she thought, for there, sitting in the chair by her bed, his head bent over a book, was the still figure of her consultant. As she looked at him, her vision still blurred, he raised his eyes and met her startled gaze. She must be dreaming still, she reasoned to herself. Yes, surely so, for he had taken off his mask and everyone in her waking world wore mask and gown.

'I thought I'd wait for the results on your CSF,' he said mildly.

'I *am* dreaming!' Dido was not sure if she spoke the words out loud or merely thought them with exceptional clarity. The dream-like figure continued to read from the small volume in his hands. She continued to gaze at him in a kind of wonderment. However many times she had seen him she had never taken for granted his dark good looks. Dido looked again at his clear cut jaw, the straight nose, the distinctive profile she had first glimpsed that night he almost ran her down in an incident that seemed a lifetime away. For Dido felt that she had known and loved James Dauntcey all her life.

Then as she looked at him through her half-closed eyes, Dido realised he had stopped reading and was watching her from under his dark lashes.

'What are you reading?' Dido asked in a dreamy, far-away voice. Was it possible to have a conversation with a figment of one's imagination? she wondered, her thoughts disjointed by the fever that still gripped her. But yes, indeed, the vision of the man she loved began to speak.

'One of Shelley's lesser-known poems. Do you want me to read it to you?'

Dido nodded and slowly he began to read in a hushed voice.

> '*Yet look on me—take not thine eyes away,*
> *Which feed upon the love within mine own,*
> *Which is indeed but the reflected ray*
> *Of thine own beauty from my spirit thrown . . .'*

His voice tailed off as he raised his eyes to Dido's face. Through the confusion of her fevered brain those quietly spoken words drew her heart like a moth to the flame. As it was only a dream, she felt brave enough to slowly extend her hand. Lovers in dreams had no taboos. His fingers brushed hers, then closed about them with a warm intensity.

'I love you,' he whispered, shocked even by the boldness of his own words. The lateness of the hour and the quietness of this small room where he was closeted with his beloved angel had dissolved the usual inhibitions and constraints that bound him. He did love her—how natural to tell her so.

But to Dido, that whispered declaration meant it could only be a dream, and in her dream she squeezed his hand and smiled with her whole heart in her eyes.

'I . . .' she began to tell him she loved him too but her words were interrupted by the sharp click of the door as it opened, and suddenly Dido was fully awake.

Staff Nurse Williams stood in the doorway. 'Dr Dauntcey, CSF results. All's clear.'

'Good. We're saved that worry, at least,' he said briskly, picked up his book and promptly left. 'Goodnight Miss Alexander,' he called over his shoulder. He added to Julie Williams as he passed, 'Would you change Miss Alexander's linen? She's very feverish and cool clean sheets will make her feel better. I'm off to bed.' And he closed the door softly.

Dido felt quite bereft at Dr Dauntcey's going. How empty the bare room seemed without his larger than life presence. Mechanically, she climbed out of bed so that Julie could strip off her damp sheets and replace them with crisply laundered ones. Julie walked into the room brandishing a clean nightgown as well, so Dido stood

meekly like a child as she lifted off her old gown and
slipped the clean one over her head.

'Has your vision improved, Di?' Julie asked solicitously.

'Yes, I think so. It's still a bit blurred, but I'm no
longer seeing two of everything.' Dido climbed weakly
back into the high bed, grateful for the little push Julie
gave her.

She lay between the cool sheets in the twilight cast by
the corridor light outside her door. If only it hadn't all
been a dream, she thought longingly. If only James
Dauntcey had really said he loved her. If only there was
no Lady Dauntcey, then she would really believe that
dreams could come true.

CHAPTER NINE

'YOUR MOTHER is coming up this afternoon to see you.'
Millie had walked into Dido's room carrying a tray with
a syringe on it. 'That's the good news, now for the bad.
Injection time.'

Dido had had a fitful, dream-ridden night but felt less
fragile and feverish once daylight filtered through the
hospital blind hanging at her window. She obediently
rolled over onto her side so that Millie could inject
her.

The familiar sweet smell of ether filled the room as
Millie swabbed her skin. Then followed the stinging pain
as the streptomycin was injected into her muscle.

'Ouch!' Dido exclaimed. 'I'd expect a friend to be
more gentle.'

'What do you mean?' Millie said in mock indignation.
'I couldn't have been gentler! As you know, it's the
antibiotics which sting so much.'

'I know. I'm sorry.' Dido smiled as she rolled over
onto her back again. 'How was my mother? Not too
upset by the news, I hope.'

'No, she was marvellous. Said, "I always warned the
girl against nursing. Never know what nasty things you
might pick up!"' and they both laughed.

'The mind boggles! What do you think she's afraid of
us nurses picking up—undesirable males, perhaps?'
Dido laughed again and then started coughing.

'Come on, Di. Not too much hilarity. Talking about
undesirable males, I wonder how your mother would

163

class your dishy Dr Dauntcey?' Millie immediately regretted her words as she saw Dido's face fall.

'He's not my Dr Dauntcey. I'm not smitten, not any more,' she added wistfully. 'Not since I met Lady Dauntcey.'

'Not his mother!' Millie sounded shocked.

'No, his wife.' Dido's voice was bleak.

'Oh no. I am sorry, Di. What can I say?' She came over and sat on Dido's bed, her mischievous eyes suddenly subdued and smiling sadly over the top of her mask.

'Thanks for *not* saying you told me so. I feel such a fool. And last night I had the clearest dream in which he read me poetry and said he loved me.'

'Oh Di, it must have been a dream. I have yet to meet a doctor who reads poetry!' Millie's irrepressible sense of humour was beginning to rear its head again.

'I know.' Dido could not help smiling too, at her joke. 'But you can't imagine how much I longed to believe it was real.' Dido's pale face looked so forlorn, Millie involuntarily put out a hand to squeeze hers.

'Even if it did happen and wasn't a dream, it doesn't get rid of the wife, does it love?' she said softly.

'Oh, Millie, why is love so painful?' Dido's eyes were full of anguish.

'Because then it's all the more worthwhile in the end. If it was easy we wouldn't want to know.'

'Oh, you old cynic. You wait till you fall in love.' Dido sighed and closed her eyes.

'I have.' Millie's words were so quiet and unemphatic that it took a few seconds before Dido realised their full implication.

Despite her weakness, she sat up and propped herself on an elbow. 'Millie, who?' her voice was quite hoarse and squeaky with surprise.

'Well, actually it's Frank. I hope you don't mind,' Millie said in a rush and then looked anxiously at her friend.

'Mind? I'm delighted! I don't know two nicer people. How did it happen?'

'Oh, you know Frank and I've known each other for ages, and always been good friends. But since I've been in charge of your ward and been working with him, something special's happened between us. I suppose love's just grown, that's all.'

'Well, it's marvellous news and it's cheered me up no end.' Dido sank back on her pillows, smiling despite her utter exhaustion.

'Sleep now, Di. You mustn't be all washed out when your mother comes this afternoon.' Millie tiptoed away, closing the door very quietly behind her.

'Hello, darling.' A warmly familiar voice roused Dido from sleep. Although she too was wearing a mask and gown, her mother's face and figure were unmistakable. Mrs Alexander was a tall, impressive woman whose luxuriant red hair was now a dignified white, all the more striking in contrast to her recent tan. She sat in the chair beside Dido. 'I can see I needn't have brought any flowers,' she said, smilingly indicating the overflowing vases of roses and lilies.

'I still don't know who sent them,' Dido said musingly.

'Well how are you, my poor darling?' Mrs Alexander peered closely at her daughter and was reassured to see she looked much the same, apart from her pallor and thinness.

'I'm feeling better than yesterday, thanks Mum. I hope I'll be out of here in a week.'

'Well, then you'll be home to convalesce, with your

father and me to look after you. But, darling, what exactly is TB? The name has such dreadful associations I almost dropped the phone when your friend Millie told me.'

Dido smiled and patted her hand. 'You don't need to worry. I've got pulmonary tuberculosis which means the infection is only in my lungs, and according to the X-ray they took yesterday only in a small section of my right lung. You're right, untreated, the disease can have devastating complications and even result in death. But the drug treatments given these days are almost invariably completely effective. It's not even as infectious as it was once believed to be.'

'Good! I couldn't bear to have to walk around the house dressed up like this while you're staying. And your father would have a fit!'

'Did you see Millie on your way through?' Dido asked her mother, eager that they should like each other.

'Yes, I did. A very nice girl, I thought. Sensible and down to earth. She introduced me to a tall, good-looking doctor. It's funny he should turn out to be a Dauntcey—you know the estates that lie to the south of our house, that's all Dauntcey land.'

Dido's heart had started to beat in a disconcerting fashion. Her mother and Dr Dauntcey had already met! Why did Millie have to introduce them, she thought with irritation. She gazed directly into her mother's eyes to see if she could read any unspoken thoughts there. She knew her mother so well, and *she* no doubt knew her daughter even better. It would be hard to keep much from her.

'How do you know this Dr Dauntcey is the same family as the Dauntceys of West Moleshill Court?' she asked as nonchalantly as she could.

'Oh, we got talking. When Millie introduced me as your mother, he asked where we lived and when I said Wiltshire he told me his family had land down there. Suddenly the penny dropped. He says he sometimes goes down for the shooting and riding, although he hasn't gone down there much recently.' Her mother was smiling perfectly innocently.

'You seem to have got on like a house on fire,' Dido said a little sourly.

'What's the matter, darling, don't you like him? He was terribly complimentary about you. Said you were the best nurse he'd ever worked with and that he was personally in charge of your treatment.'

'That's nice of him.' Dido was feeling rather resentful but she did not quite know why.

'Anyway, he said he'd like to come and see us while we've got you at home convalescing. He'd like to check on your progress.' Mrs Alexander looked pleased as she smiled openly at her daughter.

'Mum, he's married! I know what you're thinking, but there's no point in indulging in any matchmaking fantasies in that direction!' Dido's voice had risen in tone and her mother looked at her shrewdly.

With a mother's instinct, Mrs Alexander realised that this was a painful area of discussion for her daughter and it would be best not to question her further but to shrug it off lightly.

'Darling, I'm not matchmaking for a minute. I just thought he was a nice man and a good doctor and how thoughtful to say he'd drop in and see you if he's up at the Court for a weekend. He only said he might,' she said reasonably.

'Oh, Mum, I'm sorry to be so rude. I'm just tired and I feel rather lousy. It *is* lovely to see you and I'm so grateful to you for making the journey up to town straight after your holiday and all. Oh, I haven't even asked you about that! Did you and Dad enjoy yourselves?' Dido was contrite over her bad-temper and selfishness and her heart went out to her mother for her unfailing wisdom and understanding.

'We had a lovely time, thank you, darling. We swam every day, ate terribly well, did some sight-seeing. We'll be able to show you our photos when you come down to stay.'

They both looked up as the door opened and Dr James Dauntcey, masked and gowned, walked into the room.

'Ah, Doctor, I was just going.' Dido's mother stood up and, unable to kiss her daughter, squeezed her hand instead.

'Before you go, Mrs Alexander, I just wanted to ask you if it would suit you if I discharged your daughter into your care at the end of the week. That is, if she continues to make good progress.' He stood by the door, his hands thrust deep into the pockets of his jacket.

Dido's mother beamed him a smile. 'Of course, Dr Dauntcey, I'd love to have her as soon as possible.'

'Well then, I'll ring your GP down there. I know him well, of course, he's my family doctor too. I'll acquaint him with Dido's treatment. Really, these days, if the patient's feeling up to it there's no reason why she shouldn't be up and about, doing everything she'd normally do,' Dr Dauntcey said as he held the door open for Mrs Alexander to pass through.

'See you at the end of the week then, darling,' she waved and walked through into the main ward.

James Dauntcey walked over to stand beside Dido, looking down at her reflectively. Dido blushed slightly under such scrutiny and pulled the sheet up over her old hospital gown which had a habit of gaping at the front.

'I think you'll recover your strength quicker in the country under your mother's excellent care,' he said, his eyes serious and intent on her face. 'We'll all miss you terribly, but I think it's the best answer for you. As long as you're scrupulous about taking your drugs.'

Dido was caught in a maelstrom of conflicting emotions. There was no doubt that she wanted to get better as quickly as possible and she looked forward to going back to her family home for a few weeks' rest, but she could not bear to think of leaving her friends and her job, and most of all Dr Dauntcey, the man she loved despite the dictates of common sense.

Although she knew it was hopeless and one-sided and at the worst could only lead to a cheap fling, which did not interest her, Dido felt sustained by her almost daily contact with him. How could she live without that, she wondered.

Dido had not answered and Dr Dauntcey sat down beside her, concern in his eyes. 'You *are* feeling better, aren't you?' he asked solicitously.

'Oh yes,' Dido said hurriedly. 'I was just thinking, that's all. I'll be happy to go home whenever you think it's advisable.'

She looked so heart-wrenchingly beautiful, her cat-like eyes huge and dark in her pale face and her russet hair strewn out over the pillow. Dr Dauntcey could not meet her eyes for a moment. He looked instead at her hands which lay, folded together on the white sheet, like two birds, a symbol of such vulnerability and innocence that he was prompted to express out loud the thought that tormented him.

'I dread losing you. I'll miss you terribly!' The words

were spoken in a rush as if he was embarrassed at revealing even a little of his feelings. He took a deep breath and continued, 'I'll be down at West Moleshill and I'd like to take you out to dinner to celebrate your recovery.'

Dido's emotional turmoil increased unbearably as she heard the very words she had longed to hear spoken. But now she knew the circumstances were all wrong. She did not want an affair with a married man. It had always been one of her rules and was never more important than now—for she was actually in love with the man. She knew it would be disastrous to break that rule.

To mask her emotions, she said rather stiffly, 'I don't think that would be advisable.'

Dr Dauntcey looked puzzled and then quite withdrawn and hurt. 'What on earth do you mean?' He had revealed a secret part of himself to her and she was coolly rejecting him as if his vulnerability had cost him nothing.

Dido knew that it sounded as if she was snubbing him cruelly, throwing his show of emotion back in his face, but she was afraid of entering dangerous waters by allowing herself to grow any closer to him.

'It's just that, given the circumstances, I don't think we should go out together.' Her voice sounded small and prim.

Dr Dauntcey's hurt had turned to anger. 'What circumstances, dammit? Have you got a boyfriend hidden away in the country, or is a consultant who's mad about you not good enough for you?' He had sprung to his feet, his navy blue eyes flashing with a potent mixture of fury and dismay.

Dido felt quite intimidated by his angry presence. Then she felt indignation rise in her, too. How could he think she would be the sort of girl to embark on a little dalliance with a married consultant, however rich, good-looking and successful he may be?

Dido sat up in bed to make her words carry more weight. 'No, I have not got a boyfriend in the country. It's *your* circumstances which bother me. You've picked the wrong girl, Dr Dauntcey! I have some principles and I think my abiding by them will mean we'll both be happier.'

Her heart was hammering with her own hurt pride but then, as the pain and disappointment surfaced, her anger trickled away and she slumped back against her pillows. It had been difficult to turn him down. She could have pretended for a night that he was free, that he could be hers to love and to hold. But experience had taught her wisdom. She knew that, having given herself to him heart and soul, the reality would seem all the more cruel.

Dido glanced nervously at James Dauntcey and was surprised to see him look so puzzled before he became toweringly angry again.

'I've never heard anything so priggish in my life! You're right, I have picked the wrong girl.' He stormed out of Dido's room, sharply closing the door behind him.

The journey down to Wiltshire lifted Dido's spirits a little. The November cold had dusted everything with a hoar frost and the silver filigree of the bare trees stood out against the rolling downland spread on either side of the motorway as Dido's father drove them home. Dido, dressed in her warmest clothes, sat in the back of the car gazing out at the landscape before her, her brain teeming with uncomfortable thoughts.

Everyone had seen her off from the hospital. Millie and Anne Bradshaw and Julie, her junior nurses, Frank and Russell—all had dropped in to say goodbye. She had found herself looking hopefully towards the door, hoping against hope that a familiar tall dark figure would come to wish her well, but she knew she could not really expect it, and Frank had warned her that Dr Dauntcey was caught up with an emergency on Hartland ward.

Frank had given Millie such a fond look that Dido felt her heart ache. She wanted to be gazed at with such longing. Not by Frank, of course, for she could not be happier that he and her best friend had got together, but she felt a desperate sadness that she seemed always to fall in love with men who could not reciprocate her love.

Unseeing, her eyes rested on the empty fields, their ploughed furrows frozen into motionless waves, and she thought of the emotional desert her life seemed to have become. Perhaps she ought to apply for a year's work abroad, just to break the mould and give her a change of social scene?

As they left the motorway, Dido was roused from her reverie and looked for the familiar landmarks of coppice and pub.

'Dad, you've taken the wrong turning, haven't you?' she asked her father as she searched in vain for some feature she recognised.

'No, darling, it's just a different route home. We take it sometimes for the sake of variety,' Dido's mother answered her soothingly, turning round to check that her daughter was surviving the journey. 'Are you still all right? Not too tired?'

Dido felt a little pale and wan but she knew that was only to be expected on her first day out of hospital. She nodded, smiling, and looked out with curiosity on the unfamiliar landscape. It was a beautiful part of the country, an area she had not visited before. The scale was smaller and prettier than the great rolling downland she knew so well. Suddenly her attention was caught by an ornate gate-house and the beginning of a stretch of monumental stone wall.

'That's pretty,' Dido said, craning her neck to see better the Gothic gate-house which, with its arched windows and soaring eaves, looked like a classic gingerbread house.

'Oh, that's the east entrance to West Moleshill Court, the Dauntcey estate,' her mother said nonchalantly. A frisson of excitement made Dido shiver involuntarily, and then a dull depression descended upon her. Even travelling a hundred miles from the hospital she could not free herself of associations and memories of him. Her childhood home abutted Dauntcey land, was probably once owned by his family; the only escape was to go abroad, she told herself bleakly.

As the road followed the curve of the impressive stone wall, Dido's natural curiosity reared its head. Walls had always fascinated her. They were mysterious and intriguing, enclosing secret gardens, magical houses, forgotten ruins. She always longed to find what lay within them.

'Who lives at the Court now?' she asked her mother.

'I think there's the old dowager, and her children come down occasionally.'

'How many children?' Dido asked, suddenly unconcerned as to whether she was showing excessive interest, given her protestations to her mother that Dr Dauntcey was merely a colleague.

'Well, I'm not sure. There are two brothers I think, one of whom must be your Dr Dauntcey, and perhaps a sister. Or did she die in a hunting accident? I really don't know for sure, I'm afraid. But Mrs Pargetter down in the village knows everything about the family. She used to work up at the Court when she was a young woman.'

Suddenly the line of the wall broke to reveal a beautiful main entrance lodge and great wrought-iron gates. Dido's father brought the car to a halt opposite the gates so that they could all get a better look.

Dido gasped. 'It's magnificent!' She gazed through the filigree of the gates up the oak-lined drive towards a pale stone mansion that sat, flanked by dark trees, on the brow of a hill.

'It's pretty enormous just for one elderly lady. All the locals hope that a young family will live there again.' Dido's mother's expression was one of pure innocence, but Dido gave her a sharp look. She did not believe she had relinquished her romantic aspirations involving the Dauntcey family and her beloved only daughter.

Within a quarter of an hour they were home and Dido was being greeted enthusiastically by Roddy, the family retriever. She looked with affection on the comfortable Georgian facade of her family home. It had once been a vicarage and had all the solid, spacious symmetry of that enlightened age. Its face only changed with the seasons and their effect upon the creepers and shrubs that grew against its enduring stone.

Dido loved this constancy. She knew that her room would be just as she had left it, soft and chintzy with gently faded linen curtains. Her kidney-shaped dressing-table which she had been so proud of as a girl, would be standing by the window with its skirt of rose-sprigged cotton, just as she remembered it when she first saw it ten years ago. Her old teddy, with the battered ear, would be tucked up in bed with Gregory Peck, her equally old and loved penguin.

Dido walked into the hall and smelt the familiar cool,

polish-scented air. The floor was old flagstones, partly covered by her parents' fine collection of Persian rugs.

'Welcome home, darling. Have a cup of tea, and then how about bed?' Dido's mother put her arms round her and gave her a hug.

The days merged one into the other. Dido got up late, ate well of her mother's excellent home cooking and helped a little in the garden, although there was very little to be done at that time of year. Every afternoon she took Roddy, the retriever, for a walk through the woods that flanked her parents' land. It was an event both Dido and the dog looked forward to enormously. It gave Dido a perfect opportunity to think clearly about her life and plans as she strode through the undergrowth, investigating fox holes and on the lookout for any signs of badgers. Roddy ran on ahead of her, following interesting scents, rushing off on a trail and then gambolling back to her, his tail wagging furiously, his nose muddy and pink with excitement.

During these convalescent days, Dido also had time to read a great deal and was enjoying all the novels she had promised herself as an off-duty treat but had never got round to. She spent her days in apparent contentment. But not far beneath that serene exterior, the pain and emptiness in her heart was like a wound which could not heal.

Millie rang occasionally to talk and Dido was delighted to hear her jolly voice relating hospital gossip, but it all seemed a world away. She never once enquired after Dr Dauntcey and Millie never once volunteered, although in conversation she had mentioned how subdued Dr D was and Dido's heart had missed a beat.

An old boyfriend of Dido's, who had inherited his father's farm and become a farmer, invited her over for supper with a couple of their mutual friends. They had had a lovely evening sitting in the old farmhouse kitchen, the room lit only by the roaring open fire. He had cooked a delicious meal of pheasant, shot on his own land. They had all eaten extremely well and laughed a lot. exchanging memories of their time together as teenagers and anecdotes of what had befallen them since. For a short while, Dido could forget the heartbreak, the one man for whose presence she longed. For a moment she could bask in memories of the past and the affection of old friends.

But then, driving herself the mile and a half home, the full implication of her situation was borne in on her. The velvety blackness of the night enveloped her and her little car. She was the only person on the road and no other sign of life, no light from house or vehicle, impinged on the darkness.

Dido felt her isolation and loneliness so keenly that a stifled sob escaped from her throat. She hurriedly turned on the radio for company, but the car was filled immediately with the haunting melody of Bruch's violin concerto, the most poignant sound she could imagine. Quickly, she snapped it off. It was more than she could bear.

Then at last the lights of her parents' house twinkled to her from just round the next bend. A snowy owl swooped eerily across the road in pursuit of some small furry creature, and it was with an overwhelming sense of relief that Dido turned the car into the gravel drive and come to a scrunching halt by the front door.

The next day was a Saturday and it dawned clear and bright. Dido woke up early and watched for some minutes the stream of morning sunshine shaft through the gap in her curtains. Her door was nuzzled open and suddenly Roddy was on the bed, wagging his whole body apologetically, whimpering ingratiatingly and gazing at her with dark, limpid eyes.

'I know you want a walk. Well, you'll have to wait five minutes while I dress.'

Dido scrubbed his head affectionately with her fingers and got slowly out of bed. She walked to the window. Although the sun poured out of the sky, it was still surprisingly cold and the dark shadows cast by trees and shrubs in the garden were sparkling white with frost.

Dido slipped into a long-sleeved lacy vest and then donned her thickest corduroy trousers, a wool shirt and two jerseys. Roddy was waiting patiently by the door as she quickly dragged a brush through her hair and tied it back with a pink ribbon that was handy. Then her padded husky waistcoat, gloves, her father's old hat and her smart green wellies completed her cold-beating outfit.

'Come on, Roddy,' she called as she set off towards the field at the back of the house, breathing the icy air deep into her lungs. White plumes of steam swirled from their nostrils as both girl and dog set off towards the distant woods.

Dido enjoyed this walk. She usually kept to the grassy rides which intersected the dark, dense woodland while Roddy went off on his own, exploring anything which caught his doggy attention. Dido thought this woodland probably marked the boundary of Dauntcey land and that technically she might be trespassing, but she had always walked here, ever since she was a girl, and had never been warned off. Roddy, too, was well-behaved and rather cowardly and unlikely to cause any damage to land or living creature.

They had gone about a mile. The sun was just slanting its golden light through the trees, illuminating patches of brilliant green moss, the occasional old badger set, lichen-covered stumps and ivy and wild strawberry. Roddy had disappeared from view and Dido strolled along, breathing the sweet smell of leaf-mould on the air.

Then in the distance she heard the unmistakable drum of horses' hooves. Dido could not tell from which direction the sound came, only that it was getting louder. In the silence of the morning the insistent beat of those galloping hooves seemed more than a little sinister and threatening. Dido knew that the worst that could happen was that she would be reminded she was trespassing and be politely asked to leave. Nevertheless, her heart started to beat a little faster with apprehension.

Suddenly the sound was behind her. She turned and let out a little suppressed cry as she saw an enormous black horse and rider careering towards her down the sun-lit ride. Dido was rooted to the spot, unable to leap aside even if she had wanted to. The rider expertly brought his panting, snorting steed to an abrupt halt in a shower of mud.

'You're trespassing!' he bellowed, steam curling from the nostrils of both horse and rider.

'I live near here. I've always walked in these woods since I was a girl,' Dido answered back. She did not care for being talked to so brusquely, even if she were technically in the wrong.

'Oh, I beg your pardon. With that hat on I thought you were a youth.' The rider sounded apologetic as he dismounted. 'We've had some trouble with poachers now that it's getting near Christmas.'

Even though the sun was still behind him and Dido

could not properly make out his features, the voice and the height and general build of the man were thrillingly familiar. Suddenly he too knew that beneath that man's hat was the beautiful angelic face which had haunted his waking and sleeping hours.

'Dido, my darling girl!' In two strides he reached her and, without any further ado, swept her into his arms. Her exclamation of surprise was silenced by his urgent mouth on hers. The pressure of his warm, hungry lips was such an insistent demand for surrender that Dido had no will to resist. She gave herself up to the embrace. Her own long-denied passion surged through her body as her arms slid around his neck.

She felt she was blissfully drowning in his kiss. Dido lost her sense of being separate as her soft body cleaved to his. At last she emerged, dazed and swooning from his kiss, but his arms still held her so tightly she could feel his steely forearm locking her against his broad chest, his riding-coat buttons hard on her breasts.

'You can't imagine how much I've longed to do this,' he said fiercely, looking down at the woman captive in his arms. 'Thoughts of you have filled my days and dreams of you haunted my sleep. Can't you see how haggard I've grown through lack of your healing presence?' And he bent his head and gently rubbed her nose with his.

'Oh, James,' Dido sighed, his name coming easily to her lips, for she had whispered it many times as she lay on the verge of sleep. 'I've been . . .'

Her words were interrupted by his lips tracing their intimate path along the nape of her neck. Dido shivered with delicious anticipation. His kisses followed a line from the most sensitive piece of skin behind her ear to her jaw, the curve of her cheek, and eventually found her mouth again in an unmistakable expression of his desire. Dido's body arched against his as his hand moved down to press her hips against him. She felt her desire rise to match his.

Afraid of where it might all lead, she broke away from his embrace. They gazed at each other in wonder, their eyes dilated and brilliant with emotion. Dido thought how different James Dauntcey looked in the soft tweed hues of his hacking-jacket and jodhpurs. How handsome and tousled and youthful he was with his cheeks flushed by the cold and by passion. Dido had only seen him before in immaculate dark suits, professional, unapproachable, the archetypal consultant. Now he seemed not only more human but more rawly male. She shivered again with acknowledgement of the danger implicit in that maleness.

Dido's hat had fallen off and her hair had become loosened and wild. She looked all the more fragile and desirable in her big bulky clothes and baggy corduroys. Her delicate white neck and slender hands were, in contrast, finely drawn and touchingly feminine. And her glorious hair was set alight by the slanting rays of the sun.

'I was going to come and see you tomorrow. I've got a surprise . . .' He turned at the sound of approaching hooves and Dido swung round to look too.

A man and a woman on bay horses cantered up towards them. The woman called out, 'James, we've been looking for you everywhere.'

Dido recognised her at once. How could she ever forget that perfectly-groomed beauty, those imperious dark eyes? Shock, hurt and anger combined in a confused and overwhelming emotion which sent Dido's head reeling. How could he compromise her like this?

How dare he cause her so much pain! But oh, how much she loved him. Her brain was bursting with the strain of so much raw emotion. Her face was sheet white. Dido barely noticed the second rider who was silhouetted against the low sun.

Through the booming in her head, Dido heard James's distant voice.

'Dido, this is Olivia, whom I think you've met, and this is my brother, Hugo.' His words died on his lips as he turned to see Dido crumple to the ground.

'Oh no!' he gasped and fell to his knees beside her. He glanced up at his brother and Olivia, his face an expressionless mask. 'She's been very ill. I'll get her home. You ride on.' James Dauntcey rapped out his words and then turned his head to hide his emotion.

As he gently held Dido's wrist to check her pulse, he gazed on her beautiful, serene face, his own heart racing with fear and desire. He stripped off his hacking-jacket and made a pillow for Dido's head. The doctor in him knew that she had most probably only fainted, but the man in him was gripped by a terrible fear that there was something more serious wrong. He could not live without her; he had known that for some time but now, her body stretched pale and unconscious before him, the thought was filled with dread.

James Dauntcey tenderly brushed a golden tendril of hair from Dido's forehead just as she opened her eyes. 'Thank God,' he whispered to himself.

Dido felt she was climbing out of a black tunnel into brilliant light. She was gazing up at the sky through the bare branches of trees. Then she saw James' face, dark, tender, concerned and devastatingly good-looking. The flood of painful emotions once more enveloped her but it was anger which she expressed to him.

'How *could* you?' She tried to transmit the vehemence she felt but her voice was still weak. Dido struggled to sit up, swaying slightly with dizziness. James Dauntcey put an arm round her shoulders to help her to her feet. She tried to shrug his arm off. She was hurt and humiliated at having been caught in his embrace by Lady Dauntcey and angered that he continued to treat her so intimately.

'What sort of a fool do you think I am?' she whispered through clenched teeth as she stumbled to her feet.

James Dauntcey wordlessly took her arm and led her to his horse. His face was stern but a small wrinkle by his left eye twitched in amusement. He did not know what she was ranting on about but his relief at her rapid recovery made his spirits soar.

'I'd better go home now,' Dido said coldly, looking around for her dog, Roddy.

'I will drive you home in good time. But you're coming up to the Court first. I want to make sure you're all right.'

Dido was angry again. 'I'm not going to your house, I'm going home,' she expostulated and started to walk off through the woods. This man's arrogance and insensitivity knows no bounds, she thought to herself as she climbed over fallen logs and ducked hanging branches.

Dido still felt weak and rather dizzy. Suddenly she nearly lost her balance completely as her arm was caught and held in a firm grip.

'I'm not having you collapsing in the woods and not being found until morning. You're coming with me.' James Dauntcey's voice was quiet yet as firm as a rock and Dido knew instinctively that if she argued any more she would be unceremoniously picked up and slung over his shoulder. With bad grace she turned and followed his tall, striding figure back to the path where his horse stood patiently cropping the grass.

Without uttering a word, he offered his hand for her boot and effortlessly lifted Dido into the saddle. Then, putting his arm round her and grasping the pommel, James vaulted astride his horse to sit behind her, his arms encircling her as his hands took up the reins.

'West Moleshill Court is just at the end of this ride. It's a shorter and easier journey than to your house. But I promise I'll drive you home immediately.'

Dido was disturbed by his peremptory manner but she was even more disturbed by the proximity of his body. His arms pressed against the sides of her breasts as he controlled his horse with the reins. Her back was hard against his chest and the warmth of him spread through her like the sun. His breath on her hair, his looming presence, all made her long to turn her head and kiss him passionately once more. But he was married!

The thought kept hammering in Dido's brain. He was married to Olivia, that sophisticated beauty, so much better suited to him than she could ever be, with her unruly mane of hair and her freckles and her flecked amber eyes.

Then, following the turn in the track, there through the trees ahead of them lay the spectacular Elizabethan mansion, its rosy stone glowing pink in the winter sun. Dido had never seen it close-to and was amazed at its size.

'It's beautiful, isn't it?' James Dauntcey said softly into her hair.

'Yes, it is. But what an enormous place.'

'Ah, you'll get used to it,' he said as he dismounted. Dido was just wondering what that oblique comment meant when James put both arms up to her, grasped her firmly with a hand on each side of her waist, and swung her to the ground.

Dido attempted to smooth her hair down a little and tucked its unruly curls behind her ears. She suddenly felt self-conscious about the state of her clothes, chosen that morning for freedom and comfort rather than style.

James took her hand and led her to the front door. She removed her wellington boots and stood them neatly on the flagstone floor inside the hall. Dido looked around her in amazement. A magnificent stone staircase curved down from the gallery above. The hall itself was the size of a ballroom and dark, gleaming wooden doors led into the further recesses of the house.

James took her elbow and began to steer her towards the largest inner door. 'Come into the drawing-room. I think a drop of brandy would do you some good.'

There was a footfall above them and both James and Dido turned and gazed up towards the dimly-lit gallery where the stately, immaculately-dressed figure of Lady Dauntcey stood. Dido swallowed nervously and coloured. She longed to remove her arm from James' warm grip but he held her firmly.

Olivia Dauntcey began to descend the grand staircase, her silk skirt billowing about her slender legs. 'Ah, James. I'm glad your patient has recovered,' she said in a husky voice with a slightly transatlantic drawl. Her liquorice-dark eyes had alighted on Dido's face and she smiled.

Dido was rooted to the spot where she stood. In her stockinged feet she felt very small and unsophisticated beside this willowy beauty. She grew increasingly apprehensive and embarrassed as Olivia Dauntcey advanced towards her.

'It is Dido, isn't it?' she said sweetly, not waiting for a

reply. 'I am so pleased to meet you at last, having heard so much about you from James.'

Dido blushed. Was she being particularly clever? Were her words loaded with sarcasm? Was she trying to trap Dido into admitting some involvement? She looked at James with alarm, but he was smiling and came and took her hand, bringing it slowly to his lips.

'Yes, Dido's my special angel,' he said softly, gazing into her eyes.

Dido froze with horror. She thought Olivia and James' behaviour quite bizarre and distasteful and she did not wish to be part of it.

'Excuse me, I must be going,' she said hurriedly and turned, slipped on her boots again and walked briskly through the front door. She broke into a run as she made for the drive that led to the main road. From there she could walk home or, if she was lucky, catch a lift from a passing villager.

Although Dido was still weak, anger and misery put strength into her stride and determination into her spirit. She chastised herself for being such a fool as she walked. Fool, fool, fool; the words seemed to fall in rhythm with each step. Then as she became more tired, her spirits began to flag. How bleak everything seemed at the thought of losing James Dauntcey from her life. How tedious even her work would become without the excitement of his presence on the wards. Dido thought with irritation of how happy and self-sufficient she had been before he burst into her life. How much better off she had been then—enjoying her work and her friends and with no emotional complications.

Now, she was an emotional wreck, longing for the company, for the kisses, of a consultant, a married man, a philanderer.

Dido kicked a stone into the middle of the road and sighed; love was such a lure and an illusion. It drew one into chaos and abandoned one there. Her thoughts became gloomier and more self-pitying as she trudged along the road. She began to wish heartily that Mrs Pargetter or the postman doing his morning collection would drive past and offer her a lift.

Just as Dido was beginning to regret her precipitous exit from West Moleshill Court, a great black car silently passed her and pulled up on the road just ahead. Its looming size seemed familiar; it must be a Rolls, she thought. Dido approached hesitantly, trying to recognise the driver through the smoky glass.

The passenger door opened and all Dido could see was a man's lean hand.

'Get in. I'll give you a lift home.' The voice was calm and low and thrillingly familiar. Dido had to restrain herself from slamming the door shut on him, yet her heart made her long to throw herself into his arms.

'No thanks. I'm walking.'

'Oh come on, Di, don't be silly.' His voice was conciliatory but the overtones of condescension made her anger flare again.

'Those stupid games you and Lady Dauntcey play. They disgust me!' she said fiercely.

James Dauntcey looked bemused and said in a quiet, neutral voice, 'You've been acting rather peculiarly since you fainted. Perhaps you bumped your head as you fell.' His reasonable tone continued. 'Just get in the car, Di, and I'll take you to your home. You probably need some rest.'

Dido resented his whole approach. She sat in the passenger seat, her eyes blazing. 'It's not me who's peculiar!' she seethed.

'What do you mean?' James Dauntcey leaned towards her, his eyes intense, his manner slightly menacing.

'All that carrying on with me in front of your wife!' There, she had said it, the painful words which excluded her from happiness. Dido sat quietly and miserably by his side.

A sharp intake of breath made her turn and watch his face as it registered surprise, bemusement and then outright hilarity.

'All that carrying on in front of . . . my wife!' he spluttered the words out amid gales of laughter. 'What carrying on? What wife?' he said eventually, his eyes still crinkling at the corners with amusement.

'Well, I mean kissing me in front of Lady Dauntcey,' Dido said huffily; she could not see what was funny at all.

James Dauntcey's face was suddenly serious and his eyes darkened with desire. He put his hands on her waist and pulled her bodily towards him.

'Dido, my darling, you haven't seen anything yet,' he said quietly, but with such intensity that Dido's scalp prickled with the promise of what was to come. She felt her cheeks grow warm. She could no longer meet his eyes, for she was afraid he would read her passion emblazoned there.

'And as for Lady Dauntcey,' he said, humour creeping back into his voice, 'yes, my sweet girl, you're right, she's a beautiful, intelligent and sexy woman . . .' He paused, enjoying the startled expression on Dido's already flushed face. 'And she is contentedly married to my dear brother, Sir Hugo Dauntcey.'

Dido gasped with dismay. What a fool she had been! 'I'm sorry. It's all been a great confusion of identity. We all thought you were Sir James Dauntcey and so I took it for granted Lady Dauntcey was your wife.' Dido's words tumbled out, her voice embarrassed and apologetic. Then it slowly dawned on her that her feelings for James Dauntcey were no longer taboo, and the realisation sent her pulses racing.

'So—so, you're not married,' she stammered.

'No, and I've never had the inclination . . . until these last few weeks,' James Dauntcey added softly, cupping her face in his hands. He gazed into Dido's eyes for what seemed an eternity and Dido, mesmerised by the brilliance of those intensely blue eyes, saw passion, wonder, desire and love in their depths. Released from the constraints of the past weeks, her own love for him flooded every fibre of her body, which was suddenly warm and humming with desire.

Dido closed her eyes and urgently whispered, 'Kiss me, James, please.'

At once she was lost in the hungry warmth of his lips. Her head was pressed back against the soft leather seat and her body seemed to be entirely contained by the warm pressure of his arms.

Dido felt she was drowning in a blissful tide of heat and sensation. 'Oh, James,' she sighed, her head tilted back, revealing the white curve of her throat. His lips were tracing their irresistible path from her earlobe to the base of her neck and the pleasure was almost unbearable.

'No, no more,' Dido whispered pleadingly.

'I'll only stop if you promise me you'll marry me.' James Dauntcey's voice was muffled and thick with desire. Dido was so close to swooning she was unable for a moment to take in the meaning of his words. But her hesitation meant he once more bent his head to continue his torment, his tongue exploring the most sensitive hollow at the curve of her jaw. The tension was too much to bear.

'I'll do anything you say,' Dido moaned softly.

'Say you'll marry me then, Staff Nurse.' James's voice was imperious and demanding.

Dido straightened up and tried to look businesslike. 'Of course, Dr Dauntcey, I will,' she said. And then a beaming, ecstatic smile spread across her beautiful face. 'Is that your usual tactic for getting your own way?' she asked mischievously.

'Only with obstinate and difficult Miss Know-Alls who misjudge me, reject me and generally lead me a dance,' he growled.

'Well, I hope you realise that you took unfair advantage of an invalid. I'm still convalescent and very weak.' Dido put on a fragile, pathetic expression.

'I'm the one who was taken advantage of. From the moment we had our first row, that evening in Sister's office, I was hooked.' And they both laughed.

Dido's eyes caught sight of the clock on the dashboard. 'I'd better be getting back. My parents will be wondering where I've got to. I hope Roddy had the sense to go home.'

'Don't worry. I rang them from the house. They know you're with me and Roddy's with them.' James Dauntcey turned the ignition key and the Rolls-Royce engine purred into life. Dido sat there wondering how he knew her parents' number. He turned to her with a smile. 'I've got a surprise for you, anyway.' He looked back at the road to negotiate a bend. 'I thought your remaining convalescence ought to be spent somewhere peaceful and warm.'

'Oh, really?' Dido's eyebrows were raised quizzically.

'So I've booked you a flight and a villa in Rhodes, in an

area of outstanding natural beauty.'

Dido bridled a little. He did have an arrogant managing side and she did not like the feeling of being pushed around. Neither did she want to be packed off hundreds of miles from the one area of outstanding beauty that interested her.

'What makes you think I actually want to go to Rhodes?' she said rather stiffly.

The car turned into the drive of her parents' house and James brought it to a silent halt by the front door. He looked at Dido and smiled triumphantly. 'Because, my redheaded beauty, I've booked it for two. We're going together.'

Dido laughed in delight and amazement. 'You're very sure of your charms, Dr Dauntcey. How could you have known I'd accept?'

James Dauntcey gently took Dido's chin between his thumb and forefinger and brought her mouth to his lips. He teased her with the softest kisses, murmuring, 'You mean everything to me. I wouldn't have taken no for an answer.' He sat back with a wicked gleam in his eyes. 'Anyway, you'll soon learn that I'm always right.'

Dido's eyes widened with irrepressible glee, her smile full of mischief. 'Well, we should live happily ever after—as long as you accept that *I'm* never wrong!' They climbed out of his car laughing, and walked hand in hand into the house.

4 Doctor Nurse Romances
FREE

Coping with the daily tragedies and ordeals of a busy hospital, and sharing the satisfaction of a difficult job well done, people find themselves unexpectedly drawn together. Mills & Boon Doctor Nurse Romances capture perfectly the excitement, the intrigue and the emotions of modern medicine, that so often lead to overwhelming and blissful love. By becoming a regular reader of Mills & Boon Doctor Nurse Romances you can enjoy EIGHT superb new titles every two months plus a whole range of special benefits: your very own personal membership card, a free newsletter packed with recipes, competitions, bargain book offers, plus big cash savings.

AND an Introductory FREE GIFT for YOU.
Turn over the page for details.

**Fill in and send this coupon back today
and we'll send you**

4 Introductory
Doctor Nurse Romances yours to keep
FREE

At the same time we will reserve a
subscription to Mills & Boon
Doctor Nurse Romances for you. Every
two months you will receive the latest
8 new titles, delivered direct to your door.
You don't pay extra for delivery. Postage and
packing is always completely Free.
There is no obligation or commitment –
you receive books only for
as long as you want to.

It's easy! Fill in the coupon below and return it to
**MILLS & BOON READER SERVICE, FREEPOST, P.O. BOX 236,
CROYDON, SURREY CR9 9EL.**

Please note: READERS IN SOUTH AFRICA write to
Mills & Boon Ltd., Postbag X3010,
Randburg 2125, S. Africa.

FREE BOOKS CERTIFICATE

**To: Mills & Boon Reader Service, FREEPOST, P.O. Box 236,
Croydon, Surrey CR9 9EL.**

Please send me, free and without obligation, four Dr. Nurse Romances, and reserve a
Reader Service Subscription for me. If I decide to subscribe I shall receive, following my free
parcel of books, eight new Dr. Nurse Romances every two months for £8.00, post and
packing free. If I decide not to subscribe, I shall write to you within 10 days. The free books
are mine to keep in any case. I understand that I may cancel my subscription at any time
simply by writing to you. I am over 18 years of age.
Please write in BLOCK CAPITALS.

Name _____

Address _____

_____

_____ Postcode _____

SEND NO MONEY — TAKE NO RISKS

*Remember, postcodes speed delivery. Offer applies in UK only and is not valid to
present subscribers. Mills & Boon reserve the right to exercise discretion
in granting membership. If price changes are necessary you will be noti-
fied. Offer expires 31st December 1984.*

8DN